also by Harald Voetmann

Awake

Sublunar

HARALD VOETMANN

Visions & Temptations

*translated from the Danish
by Johanne Sorgenfri Ottosen*

 A NEW DIRECTIONS PAPERBOOK

Copyright © 2015 by Harald Voetmann & Gyldendal, Copenhagen
Translation copyright © 2025 by Johanne Sorgenfri Ottosen

All rights reserved
Except for brief passages quoted in a newspaper, magazine, radio, or television review, no part of this book may be reproduced in any form or by any means, electronic or mechanical, including photocopying and recording, or by any information storage and retrieval system, or be used to train generative artificial intelligence (AI) technologies or develop machine-learning language models, without permission in writing from the Publisher

Published by agreement with Gyldendal Group Agency
Originally published in Danish by Gyldendal in 2015 as *Syner og fristelser*

 New Directions gratefully acknowledges the support
of the Danish Arts Foundation

Manufactured in the United States of America
First published in 2025 as New Directions Paperbook 1640

Library of Congress Cataloging-in-Publication Data
Names: Voetmann, Harald, 1978– author |
Ottosen, Johanne Sorgenfri, 1986– translator
Title: Visions and temptations / Harald Voetmann ;
translated from the Danish by Johanne Sorgenfri Ottosen.
Other titles: Syner og fristelser. English
Description: New York : New Directions Publishing Corporation, 2025.
Identifiers: LCCN 2025016290 | ISBN 9780811229807 paperback |
ISBN 9780811229814 ebook
Subjects: LCSH: Othlo, Monk of St. Emmeram, approx. 1010–approx. 1070—Fiction | LCGFT: Biographical fiction | Historical fiction | Novels
Classification: LCC PT8177.32.O38 S9613 2025 | DDC 839.813/8—dc23/eng/20250408
LC record available at https://lccn.loc.gov/2025016290

10 9 8 7 6 5 4 3 2 1

New Directions Books are published for James Laughlin
by New Directions Publishing Corporation
80 Eighth Avenue, New York 10011

OTHLO OF SAINT EMMERAM (OTLOH, OTHLOH, OTLOCH, OTLON, etc.), born circa 1010 near Freising, died in the early 1070s in Regensburg. Became a Benedictine monk against the wishes of his wealthy family, primarily associated with St. Emmeram's Abbey in Regensburg, Bavaria. Dean and leader of the monastic school for a time. His most important works are the *Liber visionum* (*Book of Visions*), which deals with epiphanies, dreams, and fever visions experienced by himself and others, and *Cuiusdam monachi liber de tentationibus suis* (*A Monk's Book of Temptations*), in which he tells of theological delusions and other imminent temptations. A third work containing biographical material, *Confessio actuum meorum* (*Confession of My Deeds*), is lost. As a young man, he made an enemy of the archpriest Werinharius from Freising after he lampooned him with a cruel poem, and in 1062, conflict with the bishop, the abbot, and several of the brothers drove him to leave Regensburg and take refuge in two other monasteries until 1067. He may also have been involved in a serious case of fraud, namely the alleged transfer of Saint Dionysius's relics to the monastery in Regensburg. The writings handed down from Othlo can be found in volume 146 of Migne's *Patrologia Latina*. This book draws in part on those writings and in greater part on medieval visionary literature and hagiographies more widely.

Regensburg was home to one of the oldest documented Jewish communities in Bavaria, which endured centuries of abuse, mockery, and targeted attacks. Across from the entrance to the Jewish district, the Regensburg cathedral wall still displays a so-called "Judensau" sculpture depicting a large sow suckling several Jews. The motif exists in several variations, many of which are even more extreme. The passage about the pigsty in this book merely strives to describe a hateful artistic theme prevalent among medieval Christian communities in Northern Europe. This motif can still be found on and within German churches as a stark testament to the persecution of a marginalized population.

I have longed for divine reproach since my early youth, and ever since childhood I have begged the Lord to afflict me with throes or serious illness immediately or within days of sinning, overtly or in secret. This may be the source of my current malady.
 —Othlo of Saint Emmeram, *Book of Visions*

Mix the sweets with terrors.
 —Othlo of Saint Emmeram, *A Monk's Book of Temptations*

Visions & Temptations

Through the gruel I still saw a light

Over the course of nearly two centuries, his nails and teeth had grown through his iron gloves, his helmet visor, and the toes of his boots to form a thicket that filled the tomb from floor to ceiling, a ragged cocoon shrouding Karolus Magnus. The men who stormed the tomb, my father among them, used their swords to cut their way through, sending shards of teeth and nails slicing through the air around their heads.

From the armor and pulpy cloth they extricated the body of the man who in life had restored the earthly empire, and from whose fingers, toes, and gums this wilderness had grown. They wrapped Karolus Magnus in a baptismal gown to prepare him for his arrival in Heaven where he will rightfully be among the first to have their soulfeet washed by the Lord's servants and thereafter stand pure before the eyes of Ihesus Christ.

Son of one of the men who dressed the emperor in heavenly white

and firm in my faith in salvation

though I have merely sought to serve the Lord through singing and writing

undeserving of my salvation

I lie in the near silence I have fought so long for. I doubt my father will see the glory of the emperor in the Heavenly City.

The silence here is not yet complete, there are stains of sound, an echo of alien sounds in the silence. From outside and from below, even from above. Merely sounds of the half-perished world where we are dying. Already less real, less tangible than the clouds in heaven.

In the dark sky, a light emanates from the clouds. It is not the moon, nor the stars, but the clouds' own light, shining through their bellies from the spires of Heaven. This light from the clouds, and Recanespurch maybe shines below me.

As I fell from the bench, I pulled the tablecloth with me. Bowls, spoons, knives, chunks of bread, and all that gruel. Finally the basin toppled, sticky gruel was slopped on me, covering my face. It filled my nostrils, flooded my throat, sealed my eyes and ears.

Three brothers rose, untangled me from the tablecloth and pulled me up to sit on the bench. They had to support me as they wiped the gruel off my face, as my body could muster no strength besides coughing the stickum off my uvula.

Brother Othlo, someone said from the other end of the dining hall, as I sat gazing through the veil of cooked grain still dangling from my brows. No one had spoken before and no one has spoken since.

Rustling can be heard from above, the sound of duties carried out by those still able. Duties will always abound. Soon the congregation will shuffle toward the night stairs to Mass, perhaps

I will hear the choir below me, I must find the strength to sing along from my straw bed, anyone wishing to serve the Lord must sing to the best of his ability, merely moving one's lips is not enough.

This room has been empty for years.

Here are only the stones in the wall, the straw bed on which I'm lying, the rotting pieces of straw on the floor, the embers in the brazier. No apparitions to interpret.

There used to be hams hanging from the beam and sacks full of dried pork here, but the brothers have moved them to the infirmary where they believe they are permitted to eat bloody food without the Lord's disapproval.

It has been empty for so many years. I have passed this room every day on my way to supper without knowing it was waiting, standing empty, for me.

Through the gruel I still saw a light.

Karolus Magnus sits in his tomb in Ockhe, now wearing baptismal dress. His armor lies at his feet, his teeth and nails have started growing again. A moment after stepping into the tomb's darkness, one senses him as the source of the wilderness he has produced, a little lighter than the rest. Thus he will appear, shapeless and intangible, only slightly lighter than the dark, like a cloud in the tomb.

A brother is walking above me, dragging his feet. He is walking from the dormitory to the necessarium, another earthly duty.

I saw them move the straw in here, and three brothers carried me. One held me under the armpits, another by the legs. Wolkbart wasn't really doing any carrying, he was simply walking along with a lamp in his left hand and his right hand resting on my belly, his eyes fixed on mine. It was as though he was patting my belly while the others were carrying me.

They placed me here, and I knew then that the room had been waiting for me, that it had been left empty all these years, anticipating my arrival.

There was terror, too much terror in Wolkbart's eyes, and I would have asked him to leave me, but I didn't want to break the silence and I lacked the strength to signal to him.

He returned with a basin. I don't recall if I had fallen asleep before that. There must still have been a residue of gruel on my face, which he then washed off. I don't recall whether that terrified look remained on his face, or rather, I was not able to tell. He wrung the wet cloth over my face before carefully rubbing my cheeks and my forehead with it.

I saw the marks on the crown of his head, his pale head above me, spotted with something darker, like blotches of brain growing out of its shell to sprout on the outside, and I wondered if anyone had ever touched his brain buds, and how that might feel to him, someone touching these lumps erupting on, or through, his forehead.

He didn't have those buds or lumps when he was accepted here. Last year, or the year before that. They have sprouted while he has been with us. As though his brain has been attempting to flee the skull after he had his tonsure. The skull cracks and from the brain, gray berry bunches hatch into the world. Because his brain can't tolerate absolute confinement inside him.

I suppose no one has inquired about it, and what is there to inquire about, really.

Still, as with all apparitions, this too must be decipherable, as the Lord does not bring about such brain germination on a young man's crown and forehead for no reason. Was Wolkbart vain before coming here, and has the Lord marred his face to cure his vanity.

Mainly though, I wondered whether anyone had ever touched them, more than what their appearance signified. As he washed what remained of the gruel off my face, I wondered how Wolkbart would feel if someone touched them.

Whether poking his brain berries would reverberate all the way to his brain.

If they aren't berries, I thought, they must be a small group of brain clouds, drifting across his forehead, although I can't tell if they have moved in any direction other than forward, into the world. There is nothing in here to look at but these clouds, and for that reason alone I momentarily mistook them to be clouds made of brain.

I made the sign for berry to him by wrapping my right hand around the thumb of my left and then poking the skin under my right eye with my left index finger. How I found the strength to make the sign, I don't know. However, he had yet to learn the sign for berry. We don't usually eat berries. He merely stared at me, and now I could clearly see that the terror in his eyes remained or had returned.

I don't know for how long he stared, or for how long I continued making the sign for berry to him.

There is no sign for clouds. Our signs all signify earthly things, and no sign performed by the body can do more. We have never been able to discuss clouds during our meals. We talk of gruel and cooked vegetables and ask permission to tend to the matters of our human nature. To talk of clouds one must break the silence, which the topic fails to justify sufficiently.

Even if a sign for clouds did exist, the sign for berries would still be more appropriate. Wolkbart's brain erupts into berries, and I myself am erupting out of this world, soon grasping at it only with the tips of my nails. Bliss.

I hear Tonach, or the wind, or both. Indistinguishable.

Footfalls above me still, though farther down the corridor, approaching their destination, the doorway, where the stench of combined brotherbodily excretions seep out to stir the dormitory dreams with maleficium.

It must be Gehrwas I hear dragging his leg. He walks slowly, slower than usually. The slap of his sole, then a dragging sound followed by another slap. The low rustle of his cowl and scapular.

He didn't wait until the final moment to expel his food. Leisurely he rose to answer the call of nature, well before the need became urgent, this is how I interpret his unhurried pace. There is no rush, yet he will go to the necessarium. This is how I read the apparition.

I hear no sound from Heaven, I only sense the weak glow from the clouds. They are the color of thistle flowers. Their matte dark purple makes no stain on the surrounding sky, it is the heavenly glow itself and it doesn't lend itself to anything but the clouds.

They aren't rushing like the river, however they are moving, albeit at their own steady pace. Something the river with its roaring current could never do. Tonach lies still as it froths, beyond the town. Heaven is mirrored in its restless waters.

Lividus is the name for the color of the clouds. Like a swollen toe or the cheeks of the hanged, the blue of dead blood is called lividus.

Through the gruel I saw a light. My head can't have been submerged in gruel for very long, but it was long enough to produce several thoughts

and these gruel-encapsulated thoughts

took on a very special meaning or weight

mainly, I believe, due to their encapsulation.

They were thoughts conceived independently of senses directed at the world outside, at least a world made from anything else than a habundancia of lukewarm gruel.

The light was there, but it was neither secular nor inner, nor belonging to the glue that had me submerged. And the thoughts I mustered in this brief span of time were not prompted by the light. The heavenly glow appeared to my drowned eyes so naturally, I didn't even attach any thoughts to it. Utter bliss.

Drowning in your mother's milk must feel like this, I thought. The earth's riches have suffocated me. Comfort, caresses, and nurturing lavished on me till I could bear no more and a rift into Heaven emerged. A death utterly unlike the slashing of swords that felled so many of my ancestors

how far from a rusty blade in the belly, the blood warming the soil in a frozen field.

Nursed and spoiled to death. By what right can I cross the river to the Heavenly City. By what right can I kiss the scars and boils of its citizens, unadorned as I am by such insignia, treated gently by life until caressed to death. And still, the light appeared before me. My thoughts didn't lessen the glow, which I knew to be the distant gleam of Heaven's glory.

Not before they pulled me out of the pool by my shoulders and the brothers' soft palms had wiped the gruel from my face did this light distort and merge with light of the dining hall, where we stuff our bodies with the fruits of the earth. The red flickering of the candles. Then fear seized me.

I coughed to free my uvula of gruel and gasped for breath, the stench of burning candles, frying fat, and years of brotherly farting gave air to my lungs as precious as myrrh, hyssop, and balm of Gilead. The body fought to remain on earth, above the earth, and shamefully, I still inhabit this earth and must witness the body's struggle to hold me here.

As I saw the lights from the candles, the true light disappeared, that which I had sensed with my head deep in gruel.

Brother Othlo, said one

from the other end of the dining hall.

OTHLO or OTLOH or OTHLOH, I like the faint exhalation midway, OTHLO, and for as long as I live I would prefer that this exhalation, H, is not exhaled at the name's end as the final letter. And I would prefer not to start the pronunciation with a clear exhalation either, HOTLO, as though my name, by this initial sigh, was to convey how ancestral sin has huffed us all into existence.

But let them write OTLOH when I have passed on, and then in its written form the name itself will neatly tell the story of my fate. First a simple depiction of life in the womb, followed by a cross, a chair, a fat belly, and a final exhalation.

It all happened so fast. They filled the old pantry with straw and carried me here, Wolkbart patting my belly all the way. Perhaps to assist my digestion. He must have thought that it was digestive difficulties causing my collapse, and that he might, with repeated pats on my bloated belly, release the final O in OTLOH, ease my troubles.

He may have been right. I do feel an ache in my belly, though nothing like a blade.

I might have drifted into slumber before Wolkbart retrieved the water basin, but if so, the sleep was dreamless, and if I was awake it was without thoughts. The first thing I remember after they put me in here is the sensation of the washcloth against my face, then seeing the clouds through the window and then Wolkbart's marred face, his forehead clustered with brainberries.

This was when I made the sign to him, Berries, and I saw the terror rise in his eyes or return to them.

I no longer recall whether he appeared equally terrified when they were carrying me. Either one vision of Wolkbart has replaced the other or the visions were identical to begin with.

Nothing else has happened since I fell from the bench and had my head immersed in gruel while a light from a truer world shone above me. Nearly nothing has happened since, and not much can be interpreted from these happenings.

From above, a low murmur at first, then Gehrwas, even slower than usually, dragging his lame leg toward the privy. Hence my thought that he has not delayed the endeavor beyond the tolerable.

Even taking into consideration the labored pace always characterizing his gait, the slowness with which he now drags himself to the privy tells me that he is moving with utmost calm, experiencing no bowel pressure that can't be withstood, or it would have compelled him to move somewhat faster than his clonking footfall suggests.

Hence the thought

that Gehrwas is not struggling to keep it in. And thence a thought even worse. That Gehrwas is not headed for the privy to ease anything, but to attain some order of pleasure.

That Gehrwas finds earthly pleasure in squeezing out his dung, crouching on one of the seats that used to mark a Jew's grave and which still carries a few of these infidels' letters.

That Gehrwas awakes long before he absolutely must go, and still takes himself out there at leisure. Not wishing to hurry through this earthly deed, but looking forward to what pleasure may be had from emptying his guts through the Jew's grave marker.

That Gehrwas rises from his bed, dragging leg, cowl, and scapular, not aiming to return to the dormitory as soon as he has finished a simple and necessary undertaking, but with the clear intention of having a merry and comfortable time while his behind is dripping.

Clonk. Drag, hiss, hiss, clonk. Drag, hiss, hiss, clonk. These sounds are caused by a sinful zest, so I interpret them. Not the worst among sins, but still a hankering for the flesh and its urges.

The willful pursuit of a tingle in the body, so coveted by Gehrwas that he leaves bed for the necessarium without a dire need and in spite of the dark and the stench and the cold he must endure there. Whatever joy he presumes a release will grant him must be stronger than the discomfort it will cause him.

Hence the thought

that this pleasure, which Gehrwas knows is in store for him, is not insignificant. That he may not merely be seeking the carnal tingle of voiding his gut, but that he is lusting for other things too, or at least one other thing.

That the cripple's cock may even be standing erect as he drags himself, that he seeks to void both scrotum and gut through the Jew's grave marker to the brotherly dung heap.

Hence the thought

that Gehrwas must be stopped

before the squirtings from his cock strike our abject filth. Hence the urge to scream, but not the capacity anymore. I manage only a curious palatal clicking. Above me, far down the corridor, the presumably sinful clopping and dragging toward the privy can still be heard.

Perhaps from the duration of his visit I shall know for certain whether anything sinful has taken place, and whether Gehrwas must do penance for it. Either way, it is too late to stop him now. The cock might already be throbbing in his soft palm, grip tightening, milking the shame, after which he will drag himself back down the corridor at an even feebler pace than before, having willingly spilled a load of his life-giving fluids into the dark and the stench.

I heard a story in Tehgarinseu many years ago, of a monastery, though not the local one, where the brothers habitually spilled their seed into the privy.

And a sorcerer from the East gathered enough semen-filled dung at the foot of the slope where they emptied their latrines to create a boy child. And with God's blessing and through his chants, the sorcerer breathed soulless life into this child not born of any woman, whose very substance had been squeezed from brothers, fore and rear, so that the shit was his mass and the semen his glue.

And the sorcerer nursed and educated the child like a dear son with fine foods and heathen knowledge.

And the foul mass, from which the dung-boy had sprouted, grew skin and hair so that he appeared like a real child to human eyes. At which point the sorcerer allowed him to play freely among the children born of women in the town. Though a vague stench of excrement wafted from him, it wasn't much stronger than the stench of his peers, and it was only perceptible at close range.

Eventually, the boy was sent to the local monastery school, where the other brothers, lay brothers, and children, unaware of the boy's origin, found him to be more learned than one would expect for an orphan of his age. At the same time, he seemed familiar to them, each recognizing a resemblance like that of a father and a son.

Any brother who had ever committed adultery with one of the town whores feared that the boy was the fruit of his sin. Which he was, although it was the sin of all and not one.

However, as he was an unusually gifted scribe as well as beautiful, thanks to the sorcerer's devilry, embellishing the hideous dungball with the noblest of features, each brother felt in his fear a grain of pride as well. Were it not for the familiarity, they would have thought him a prince or the son of a saint.

And how does the story end? How I remember it, a holy man came to the monastery. When during Mass he placed his hand on the boy's forehead, the boy screamed and dissolved into his two components on the chapel floor. Without surprise or austerity, the holy man asked that the brothers muck out their filth and semen as it stank under Heaven and befouled the Lord's sanctum. The Lord had warned the holy man in a nightly vision.

So the story ends, I believe, that's all. I don't remember who the holy man was.

Perhaps Saint Severinus. Pray for my soul as death nears me.

The clouds sprout on the sky like thistle flowers in the field, billowing in the wind as though belonging to our world. They grant us on earth a reflection of the heavenly soil around their roots.

Only when the river Tonach burns will the clouds be illuminated from below. Their stalks will break under the heavenly horsemen's hooves and their blood-laden crowns will be steaming, as it has always been with thistle flower on the earthly battlefields.

The duration of Gehrwas's visit to the privy will probably not be enough for me to tell, beyond reasonable doubt, whether his intentions there were sinful. A short visit, as well as a prolonged one, could indicate either.

I consider clapping my hands together.

If Gehrwas hears my clapping, he might abstain from sin. Or if another brother hears me, he might intervene before Gehrwas concludes his pursuit.

I wonder now why I first considered screaming, in fact attempted to scream, rather than clapping my hands together.

However, now that a scream has been attempted and proven impossible, a less drastic approach is unattractive.

The fact that I managed, at great effort, to make the sign for berry hours ago when it seemed necessary, is no guarantee that I will

necessarily

at present

be able to clap.

In the Garden of the Head-Bearers

Again Wolkbart's speckled face, this time in daylight. No terror in his eyes, but maybe worry. His irises are brown, but a green snake slinks through the left one's rim. He extended a bowl of sloes toward me, he stood like that for a long time, extending his sloes, a bowl of the bitter and dark-blue fruits like the winter night itself bubbling forth from the thorny twigs. So he did read my sign after all. Or it was explained to him.

He carefully placed the bowl on the floor, put his hand on my forehead, the skin of his palm surprisingly calloused. How has this hand been put to use before he was tonsured. The brain berries on his forehead were less grayish brown than I remembered. There is a hint of rose to their tone, they are thriving, I thought.

Whether he looked more or less worried as he touched my forehead, I can't tell. But he made no sign to me before leaving and no sign of farewell.

I could cry of happiness that the Lord didn't let me scream last night, didn't allow my voice to break the silence I've kept since Heinrich left us again

if the Lord had allowed me to cry

for I have spoken to no one else since Heinrich left, used my voice only to praise the Lord and dictate.

And I wondered whether I had slept through one Mass or several. To what degree I had neglected my sacred duties.

Holy Emmeram

Dionysius

Wolfkang

Huldarigh

Gregors.

May my lips plant kisses on your crusts and sandal straps.

Where your head was severed from its trunk, Holy Dionysius, strolling among the saints in the Garden of the Head-Bearers, behind the Lord's own palace walls. Everyone there carries their own glorious head under their arm, and from their neck, where there was once an earthly wound, only lux resplendens, veritatis resplendentia æterna, now streams.

To be able to dip one's lips in the spring of glorious truth just once, to be allowed to drink the light from the stump of your neck. May my lips be cleansed in your wound for they are foul.

Intercede, Dionysius. My lips are not worthy to form the prayer. Look, they have withered in the eyes of God, not merely from what they have kissed, swallowed, and brushed, but by the insults and lies they have uttered. Withered petals in the center of my face, no human word will touch them before they have closed around the light, sucked the light and been replenished by the truth.

Today is market day in Recanespurch. They sell mountains of garbage down there, Dionysius, so much garbage. I'm not even sure why I'm telling you this. Have mercy on my blabbering, pro garrulitate veniam. The river is impossible to hear through the unintelligible yelling, which serves no other purpose than to sell more useless garbage.

Thaunistus, Thabra, Tubraham, Saturnina, Albanus, Aphrodisius. They are all there with you, strolling in their long robes, which seem to be woven with light, yet are fully covered. Each carrying their head under their arm or extending it upright from their palm. From each radiant head sounds a song of praise, though not as loudly as we must sing it here on earth.

In the Garden of the Head-Bearers, the song of praise need only be whispered, for the garden lies beneath the Lord's throne room and the joyous whisper reaches Ihesu ear through a window. May your intercession on my behalf smoothly merge with the stream and float on the harmony into the Lord's ear, so that I might find mercy this way.

There is no pain in the garden, no withering, loathing, constipation, or venom. There is no distinction between the sweet whispers from the Head-Bearers' lips, the honey springs, or the golden-beaked birds. The least rustle in the gopher leaves or the white doves tapping on a twig of myrrh are all in tune and timely in the manifold mellifluence, flowing from Creation to the Lord's dilated ear canal where hymns of praise are readily received.

There is no sin and no frown. Like happy children, the Head-Bearers toss their precious loads around between them, Thabra,

Tubraham, their blue-man faces whirling in the air, the Lord's praise a glowing ember caught tenderly between their swollen lips, Saturnina's head in flight high above the garden's trees, trailing its tail of golden hair.

Lovingly they seize, embrace, and stroke each other's precious disjoined parts. The finger of a headless body caresses the windswept hair on a temple or runs down the smooth cartilage of the ear before passing on the head to catch another, each head equally beloved by all, equally atremble in innocent joy over the game, a joy that will never cease or waver.

Holy Dionysius, Dux Ludorum, standing motionless at the center of the garden as the head game's referee, awarding gold-leaved wreaths from the garden's own trees to the players for a lucky throw or a great save, even if the wreaths will soon slide off the flying heads and end up under an anointed sandal.

Holy Dionysius, alone among the Head-Bearers, still knows grief in his salvation. For only he can fling his head high enough to catch a glimpse beyond the palace walls and in that moment of free fall, and without even losing his miter, see the scope of human sin and misery.

Did you see the raven wing of sorrow brush the corner of Dionysius's eye, my guide whispered to me. Saint Dionysius catches a daily glimpse of the human world, any more than that would cause his blessedness to evaporate and he would be too burdened to continue the game with the other Head-Bearers in the garden. The game would suddenly appear childish to him, inappropriate behavior for a saint.

He reels for a moment after looking beyond the walls. Soothes his head in his arms, caressing it to ease its agitation. Standing close enough, one can make out the head's whispering, conveying the human corruption, the sins and desires so horrendous that, were the head to speak of them in a clearer voice, the palace walls would tremble. Of fratricide and patricide, unnatural uses of women, of men sharing sinful beds and tormenting the observant angels with their embraces.

They rounded up the children in a line by the church wall, I heard the head recount. Two ruffians led the way, swinging their swords at the children's ankles, followed by two others thrusting long spears into the fallen souls. The weather was frosty, a thick mist flowed from the children's wounds and screaming mouths, but the mist couldn't shield my eyes from the sight.

In dark cellars I watched the flesh outgrow its shackles till the shackles were entirely hidden within, said the head in the holy man's embrace. And everywhere a jumble of limbs met that should never meet. They penetrated or swallowed each other till all became one in shame and lust.

And I saw a host of angels circling the sun, half of them pleading with it to not extinguish its glow in despair over the species, the other half begging the sun not to set the world aflame in anger, as none but the Lord knows the Hour of Judgment. Had these angels not been perpetually soothing the sun's despair and anger, humankind would long have perished in the cold and the flames.

I saw the powerful spread death, the peddlers spread garbage, the degenerate clergy spread poisonous lies across the Earth.

I saw the pale shreds of human flesh still hanging from the branches in the woods of ancient idols, where heathens burn Christians. The soot stained the walls of the Heavenly City and the fried stench ascended to the highest of high.

I saw the Church itself undressed, heaped with heathen dung in the clearing of an ancient god. She stood shivering and shameful, the bride of Christ, covering mammæ and pudenda, while the shit-flinging infidels scorned her.

These words too blend into the praise, reaching the ears of the great Maker. In the throne room, the Maker flinches briefly in disgust. But then the sounds from the garden overwhelm their voices, and again he hears only the trills and delight of the Head-Bearers frolicking in evergreen foliage.

Someone has replenished the brazier.

The bowl of sloes is still in front of me. The only berries to forage now. Whatever the silly brothers imagine am I to do with them.

If you could see the garbage they sell in town, Dionysius, piles of rubbish and by no means cheaper for that reason.

After a few days of paralysis, the boils and the marks under the skin begin to show. With the boils, a certain mobility returns. In case the Lord wishes to punish me but not feed me to death yet.

I can't make out the words of the peddlers' shouting, but I can tell that they have grown hoarser as the day has worn on. In the stalls and shops only the most useless or indecently priced wares remain, and though I can't make out any distinct words, I recognize the exhaustion and half-heartedness of their hawking from this distance.

Underneath the hawking, a less intelligible buzzing of the customers.

Far away, a flute trilling, which does little to praise God.

The songbirds have left us, and this histrionic's soulless imitation of their notes

makes their absence noticeable.

It is hardly the love of the Lord being piped into the instrument in rapid lurches and whirls. No note is left unspun, unturned, until the tune is nauseous, not just from motion but from itself, and after myriad spins it signs off with a faint toot and dissipates. The flute player rapidly heaves for more breath and lets out another note to be tormented to death and beyond, till its spectral state crumbles in contrived somersaults, which is how this clown has learned to exhaust ears and air.

Every market day in Recanespurch is an ode to distortion. What the flute player does to the air is what every peddler hopes to achieve with his customers' ability to think. I hear the sounds, though at a distance, praise the Lord, but louder still is the grief of the silence that must contain them. The silence roars, mournful as a church fire, around the yells and dizzy trills of greed.

Miserably, the peddlers hawk about the superior quality of their leftover mangy fox skins and chipped pisspots. Despite their brimming money boxes, they can't bear to miss out on any undeserved profit from even their lousiest remaining stock.

Soon they will close their shutters or pack down their stalls. Calculate today's profit summa cum cura, then go to Mass before a night mistreating their bodies with strong drinks and bloody foods and ejecting their despair between a whore's legs, so well trodden as to be within their stingy budget.

But throughout the night

as they send each other imposing nods by the church door, stroking the gold chains and ferret skins on their chest, thus exhibiting the rings on their fingers too

as they kneel on the costly rug they brought along in front of the poor priest, who can't possibly harbor any earnest hope of redeeming them in the Lord's eyes, as his powers are hardly that Herculean

as their tongues pry out the crumb from the body of Ihesus that got stuck in the hollow of a molar

as they descend ferociously on the abundant supper, prepared for them by death and fire

as their eyes, peeking from under the expert's frowning brows, inspect the worn orifices in their preferred price range, and as they plant their seed in whichever one they have reluctantly paid a pittance to mount

as they wobble home arm in arm on the cobbled streets, hollering songs about killing and whoring, as though those were in fact the sins closest to their hearts

their thoughts are still pivoting around the mangy fox skins and chipped pisspots that have yet to yield a profit because no simple soul has been tricked into paying their outrageous prices

the thought of numerous simple souls who, despite the peddlers' insistent hawking and lies all through market day, have yet to part with their money for these sorry goods

that is the thought that has tortured them all night and appeared to them as a sign of the Lord's fundamental injustice and persecution of their innocent souls

the injustice that ignites their holy wrath when they finally come home and see the fox skins and pisspots in the corner

then they see no other way to restore their scorned pride than to turn their wives and children into bloody pulps on the floors, the reeds of which are already blackened with bloodshed from other market days when stock remained unsold.

Soon the bells will toll and the market will close, but it will be very late before the silence is cleansed, no longer forced to contain the vilest of human traits.

The silence will never be complete. There are stains of sound in the silence, reverberations alien to the silence.

Not all sounds are alien to the silence, not all sounds are unwelcome inside it. The silence is in tune with some of them.

I sometimes long for the rush of Tonach, hidden under the noise of the market. Merely so I can long for that sound to cease as well.

For underneath the rush of Tonach, there are no other external sounds to wish away. None apart from the sounds from our monastery, which I have attempted to minimize, and the body itself with its rushing blood and pounding heart, in tune with the silence for as long as it lasts, as long as the heart beats in praise of the Lord.

I long for the toll of the bells as it heralds the silence. And I long for the drunken, sinful songs of the peddlers because once they are over, the silence will cleanse itself of their greed and hate. I long for the songs as they are signs of their own end. We are all signs of our end. Tonight, the stream of Tonach will be the only outside sound to reach me, provided I am conscious and alive by then, and provided they let me stay in this room, Deo permittente. Then the rush of the river, alone in the world as it will be then, will serve as a reminder of its end. It is the only sound to break the silence of the world, and thus the silence of the world sings to me through it.

Until then, I must make do with flutes and hawking and the buzz of drifting customers.

The sickbed partly explained

Far below us I saw the island, though I was hard-pressed to see anything at all where my guide was pointing. A dot only slightly paler than the sea of gray, which stretched endlessly in all directions.

My heart grew heavier as we descended, and I feared it was the very weight of my heart causing us to descend from the fields eternally ready for harvest, which surround the rosy walls and pearly spires of Heaven.

For none of the peasants I had seen there knew grief

and though they aren't as blessed as the city dwellers whose food they supplied, who are closer to the Lord and who witness His glory every day when He is carried through the streets to receive the ovation

and though they only glimpse His glory at a distance, like a golden sheen among the sparkly wreaths of teeming angels

the heavenly peasants were unburdened too, and the furrows and regrets marking my face had puzzled them. Like curious children they had run their fingers along the black rims under my eyes, the slack skin on my neck, laughed about it and asked me how I had come to look so quaint. And when I answered with the words grief and hardship, they sang the words back to me as though they were a nursery rhyme

grief grief grief

hardship hardship grief

until my guide implored them to stop singing this song

but as we descended, and as I wondered whether it was the weight of my heart pulling us down, which only served to make my heart grow heavier and certainly our downward velocity to increase

the island he had pointed out seemed to grow larger, and I saw that its cliffs were grassy and had little windblown trees, and that white oxen were grazing among them.

What is the name of this island and why are we here, I asked, and my guide told me it was called Æsphydogyllus and that the two of us were going to celebrate Easter here.

The ocean is as vast as Heaven and Heaven's joy mirrors Oceani pitless grief, my guide told me as we approached the island of Æsphydogyllus from above. Just as your sorrow appears strange to the peasants of heaven, so the anguish of fish is incomprehensible to humans. None without gills on dry land can fathom the depths of despair known to fish. And since you are unaware of this misery, you casually strip the scales from its fruits and consume their pallid flesh. The last part he said at a later point.

I have been relocated to the infirmary. Three brothers carried me. One had me under the armpits, another by the legs. Wolkbart wasn't really carrying, he was simply walking along. In left hand, he had the bowl of sloes, which he still appears to think I might eat or find useful. His right hand fiddled nervously with his Adam's apple, all the way down the stairs, through the corridor, I was stiff as a board in their hands. They placed me on this bed and left me.

This is where I find myself now, as marvelous company to the infirmary's old men who despite having put duties and pledges shamelessly behind them still believe themselves entitled to salvation. There's no silence here and no lack of bloody food for the geriatrics who still have teeth to chew with. Here, I am at the mercy of their inane prattle.

Wolkbart, bent over me as they carried me. Through the skin of one particularly protruding brain berry, right below the hairline, a drop of blood is escaping. His busy fingers have been scratching it, I thought, he simply couldn't help himself.

And how did it feel, how peripherally or deeply did he feel the brainy itch, which made him scratch the berry on his forehead, perforating it with a nail, presumably

and how rough or smooth is this surface anyway, though the latter question is slightly less urgent

and how peripheral or deep was the subsequent sensation of a brain berry bursting.

And from what depths of his brain did this drop of blood originate, the drop now dangling over me, which cannot be allowed to fall, although I won't go so far as to invoke the Lord nor a saint to avoid it.

They placed me on this bed, tucked me in with two lambskins, and Wolkbart placed the bowl on my chest. Which, as it turned out, was not enough for him, or perhaps my complete lack of reaction was not satisfying to him. Because when the others had left, he pulled my arm free of the lambskin covers and tried to grasp the berries with my hand, shoveling them into my palm using my own fingers as a tool.

And this was when I noticed that the drop of blood from the ruptured and thus recognizable, in fact visibly slacker, brain berry, placed at an outer position in the rose-gray frons-cluster above me, was no longer dangling and had left no trail down the forehead either. Apparently, the drop must have fallen at some point, directly from the source, whole from the berry

onto the floor

onto the lambskins

or onto me

and in my despair over lying here among the infirmary's old men, I now despaired at this too, the drop having fallen

and my never knowing what it hit

whether this flight of the brain is contagious and has spilled onto the naked skin of my face.

It stands to reason, said my guide or companion, by whose marvelous powers I have seen both the land of the Lord and the forges of Hell, it stands to reason that you shall die or be punished on this bed, Brother Othlo. For it is in bed you have sinned the most, and the sins of the bed have always tempted you above all others.

There's a meaning to where a person is punished and meets their death. I will now explain this mystery to you, so you can be certain you're in the right place and that these punishments will not exceed what you asked for when you prayed for a fitting atonement here on earth. Whatever befalls you will only be just and right.

Since the first people brought death to the bloodline by picking it off a tree, our Savior, too, had to let himself be nailed to a tree for the Lord, to a cross made of wood to atone for the loot that caused the Fall. He hung with his arms outstretched as the arms of the first people had been outstretched reaching for the forbidden, and on the cross he had to drink the sour vinegar to atone for the sweetness that was stolen. This is just and right.

Whoever reaches for the sword must die by the sword, thus spoke Ihesus himself, and this sickbed is just as fitting in that regard. For your worst sins have taken place, if not on this bed then on other beds, or in places where lying down was possible, or simply by what is called lying. Similarly, the current stiffness of your body can be explained by the nature of the sin. You will be punished or die among blabbering old men because you have sinned thoughtlessly with young women. They too tended to gossip and blabber, though at the time, you didn't seem to mind.

The bitter sloes on your chest are, just as the vinegar, a response to the sweetness of sin, for it pleases the Lord to draw such threads through the weave of fate, allowing the sinner to read the Lord's will and wrath in his own life's apparitions and thus be inspired to repent.

This is how I interpret the apparition, said my guide. This warm, soft, and wool-covered bed is now your torture rack and your reckoning, just as the cross, before the Savior's sacrifice, was the tool with which all humans deserved to be killed.

Though I didn't feel the mystery of the sickbed had been entirely explained by his words, I could tell from my guide's facial expression that they would suffice for now, and that I must accept them as adequate. His wind-arm blew through the air, forming an arch above me.

Your eyes saw a bed covered in dirty skins. But to my eyes, the bed is adorned with pearls and jewels and it shines with precious drops of martyr blood. An angel wipes the sweat of your forehead, but you feel nothing. Another floats above your bed, his wingbeats mitigating the infirmary air, a bowl of incense dangling from his hand to clean out the stench, yet you are not cooled by his wings and the incense does not reach your nostrils. A third angel sits at the foot of your bed with golden ink and quill, ready to write an intercession for his Maker on your behalf, and the intercession will bear the seal of the Army of Angels, the Holy Emmeram's, the Holy Huldarigh's, and the Holy Wolfkang's seal, and it will be shipped to the Lord's throne room on the swiftest of wings where a choir of seraphs will sing it to the Lord, if you believe and repent.

But if you believed and repented, he continued, there wouldn't be any need for me to tell you all this, it would all be right in front of you.

Though I'm undeserving, my bed is turned away from the old brothers' part of the infirmary. I hear their words sullying the monastery silence, but I am spared the sight of them entirely. Their long gray or white beards, crumbs and bits of meat sticking out between the strands, tavern beards, which some of them wear with pride and regard as an outer sign of their tenured wisdom, something that elevates them above the flock of clean-shaven brothers. In some cases, the hair on their heads has grown out, breaking the crown of their tonsure, although some have been spared this indignity as they have grown completely bald with age, or the Lord has granted them the kind of baldness resembling tonsure. Poor old degenerates who think absolution will be theirs for the promises no longer kept, for the silences now broken, for the Masses not attended for years.

Is there onion in these sausages. I'm not having that. Anything else. Could you just try the end, then. You don't have to swallow. Maybe just cut the end off one of them and tell me if there's onion in it, and then bring me something else. The fish or the cured foods. That'll do for tonight. A bit of everything, please. No onions and no beans either. It sends my belly fluctuating. It can't be that hard. See if there's onion in it, that'd be a start. What do you think. Do any of you understand his sign, it's impossible to tell when he's holding those bowls. But you made them. You made the sausages. It's all right, you can speak here, just step over that threshold and tell me. If it's big chunks of onion. Is that what you're trying to say. Big chunks, that motion. You can pick them out of the sausages, then, I can't do that. You think these hands can leaf through a book these days. You think they can pick the onions out of a greasy sausage. I'm wondering if it's enough to remove the onions, though. There's still the juice, I mean, the onion juice that seeped into the meat, and the juice is just as troubling to my bowels, fluctuations, stomach cramps. It's pure poison to me, the juice. I'd be in cramps, and the others would have to suffer the smell and rumble, no one wants that. It's quite evident that you're not the one who has to sleep in here with me tonight. I'd prefer a hot meal, but if that's out of the question, then bring me some fish and cured meat. No, just give it to the one over there, he'll eat it when he wakes up. Shouldn't go to waste just because I can't eat it. I'm not asking for extra servings. I'm just saying there's someone over there, I really forgot his name, and he didn't get anything at all, you didn't bring him a bowl. They're sloes, I don't know what they're doing there. But he can't survive on sloes, not when he's that sick. Maybe those sloes made him sick. But you're supposed to be in charge of the infirmary. Instead of feeding my sausages to the dogs, you might want to leave them for him. Oh, you're welcome. Shouldn't have to be that hard. Well, then give him my bowl and fetch me another one, I'll manage without my usual bowl. They're all nasty anyway. Yes, that's my opinion. I've eaten out of those bowls since your mother sucked teat, long before she grew teats of her own, and every day I've been thinking, these bowls are getting worse. But isn't he going to eat anything at all. What if he wants something later. That's very thoughtful of you. The dogs will love it. Are you going to bring me some fish and cured meats. Oh. I hope they'll shit in your mouth. Enjoy it, the rest of you. I hope the dogs will shit in that one's mouth, I hope they get fluctuations from the onions and shit in his mouth. You think he'll return with fish and cured meats, or is it straight to bed hungry. Well, you won't have to listen to my farts, then, but apologies if there's a rumble anyway. It's for your sakes as much as mine. And the one in bed over there, he's not getting anything at all. Just like me. But he's not saying anything. We'll be listening to you lot chomping your sausages. I hope they agree with you. He might not love listening to it either, even if he shuts up about it. Is there onion in these sausages, is there even onion in yours, or did he just take them now and then there's not even onion in them.

I must pray for these poor souls if I ever regain my strength. There is a small window high above my bed through which I glimpse the dusky sky, undeserving though I am, the livid dusk of winter.

We landed softly on our feet on the island of Æsphydogyllus. But after all the wonders I had seen in and around the City of Heaven, our safe landing didn't seem the least bit miraculous. Blinded by the happy sights I had witnessed and my heart weighed down because I was leaving heaven, I can honestly say that as we fell to Earth, I felt no fear, only grief and regret.

My guide or companion saw my grief and whirled his airy shape around my chest in an intangible embrace. Be patient, Othlo, he said, be stronger in your faith in the Lord. We are now on Æsphydogyllus where I intend for us to celebrate Easter, and, more importantly, it is the intention of a higher will. So, he asked me to bend down and look in the grass at my feet, and in the place where he asked me to look, I immediately found a tall candle whose wick flickered aflame by the holy mystery the very moment my palm closed around it.

As the darkness fell around us on the island of Æsphydogyllus, alone in the middle of the fierce, gray Oceanus, as far from any land as from the heavenly meadows above, the two of us chanted the Easter hymn from beginning to end, he with the burning candle held high in his wind gust of a hand, and before we had finished our præcomium, the night had grown so dark around us, all I could see was the small flame burning steadily in front of my face. For despite the cold wind blowing between the cliffs of Æsphydogyllus, this flame never flickered in the least.

On this night
a pillar of light banished the shadow of sin.
On this night

Christ broke the chains of death
and rose victorious from the depths

Our birth would have been no gain,
had we not been redeemed.

To redeem a slave you gave up your Son.

O indispensable sin of Adam,
atoned by the Death of Christ

O happy sin
that gave us so glorious a Redeemer.

O most blessed night,
which alone knows the time and hour
when Christ rose from the depths.

This night
of which it is written
the night shall be as bright as day
the night shall be my light and my joy.

Amen, said my guide, and I, in the dark on the island of Æsphydogyllus, I said the same, Amen.

My guide let go of the candle but it remained floating erect in the air, for now it was hallowed and burned of its own free will. All night it burned between us as we rested on the grass. Another wonderful thing about the light was its capacity to keep me warm and dry through Easter night on this windblown island, shining as strongly as the stars on the heavendome.

My guide quizzed me about the stars, which one of these is holy, and when I didn't dare to answer, he answered himself, his voice clearly annoyed, well, even the smallest one, obviously.

The least significant of the stars is Wormwood, invisible to mortals with its black-green glow. The other stars regard it as a toad, hopping around in confusion among the black meadow's unicorns and lions. And yet, Wormwood is the star chosen to fall to Earth and spoil the waters with decay when the third angel blows his trumpet. Once the other stars recognize that Wormwood was intended for this they will honor him like the prince of all things vaguely aglow, and his place will be with the Lord.

By dawn my guide said he had to leave me for a while. Before vanishing in the air, as was his wont, he gave me the dagger from his belt and asked me to prepare our Easter feast with it, for today we break the fast with bloody foods as is tradition on this island, he said.

For the first time now I saw my surroundings clearly, Æsphydogylli cliffs and meadows and pebbled shores. In daylight, I realized that what I had taken to be grazing oxen during our descent were in fact snow-white baby lambs that were simply the size of oxen. I figured they must be sacred to the Lord and so I dared not cut their throats when they came to lick my hand, kindly bleating, tongues the size of my thigh, eyes like those of the heavenly peasants, so sacredly simple. Distraught I wandered, seeking an animal that would appear to me less sacred, yet still worthy of the airy being who had shown me the golden lands and rosy City of Heaven, and as I sobbed in my despair over my inability to find a sacrifice, the lambs gathered around me and seemed to offer me their wool to cry in.

The sun was already high when I left the meadows for the beaches with the lambs in a row behind me, hoping to find something to sacrifice.

Before our skyfall the previous day, I had never seen the ocean. And yet, among all the world's wonders, its gray endlessness seemed one of the smallest and most insignificant already, and I thought that if I never saw this monotony again I wouldn't mind.

A few steps into the water I now saw what I believed to be a seal on a rock. It had a long, pointy beak, not unlike a carrion bird's, but spotted with yellow and red, which reminded me of the market clowns and therefore repulsed me. It waved at me with a clawed flipper, a look of absolute arrogance in its dark seal eyes. Right on cue, I took this as an invitation to wade into the water and thrust my dagger thrice into its doughy belly.

On the beach I skinned, cleaned, and debeaked the beast. I flung it over the back of the most naive among the lambs, whom I had secretly named Archipresbyter Werinharius and whom I now led along to find a nice site for a fire to prepare our feast, thinking about how happy my guide would be once the fat started dripping and sputtering in the flames.

I hope they take turns shitting in his mouth from the fluctuations. That'll give him a taste of those onions.

Saint Emmeram

Saint Huldarigh

Sant Wolfkang, it would please me.

How about you?

But you didn't get any either.

Just the same as me, I didn't get any supper.

But that's because I can't eat onions.

Well, I could have eaten it easily. Would've passed the problem on to you, then. Then we'd see how you liked that gas.

I abstained out of consideration for you. Consideration for the person who'd be cleaning my behind afterward.

It's not that I didn't want it.

I hope their fluctuations have turned it into thin and plentiful sausage water.

I hope their stomachs cramp so badly they'll shit your mouths full of it.

What's the use of dogs otherwise.

Truly, I would love to see that.

But you're all just sleeping. Sleeping away from me.

Farther away, the peddlers cry their homecoming songs of blood and debauchery. The final hoarse cries from the streets before the crying starts inside the homes, followed by the silence, which, had they not moved me to the infirmary, would only have been broken by the river. The sinful hollering that might have been liberating, had I only been allowed to stay in my empty chamber. If the old brother behind me would stop blathering for a moment, the only sounds would be the rush of the river and the other brothers chewing, grunting, and snoring. As well as my own sounds, somewhat in tune with the silence. The highest degree of silence I can hope for tonight will have to include all of this.

In vain, my eyes seek the square of darkness that doesn't belong to the infirmary. Somewhere in the darkness above me, there is a square whose darkness is from the outer world, but my eyes can't tell the inside and the outside apart anymore. Define darkness. You can't distinguish darkness from darkness. A star would have disclosed it, or a light through the clouds. The darkness is as dense outside as inside, and one might think this infirmary isn't bordered from the rest, that the life and apparitions unfolding here are no less significant than what else unfolds in the half-perished world where we lie dying.

Is it vain to prefer vast darkness to the darkness one is given to and indisputably belongs to. Among all the things that stink in the near darkness, my own stench is unmistakable. It must be. A distinctive feature of this darkness. The darkness of intimate smells and intimate sounds. Heartbeats and breathing belong here too, along with the old-timer's sullen outbursts. The small square glimpse of the outside belongs here and doesn't.

Karolus Magnus sits in his baptismal gown in Ockhe, regrowing his teeth and nails into a twined cocoon around him. Karolus Magnus in his gown is somewhat lighter than the darkness of his tomb, that is how my father described it. He belongs there and doesn't. Our black robes are no lighter than the rest. We belong here, certainly.

The peddler choir, singing of the virgin Elha's sex, belongs to the outside. Listen, little sex of mine with the golden sparrow down. The request, the reply, and then the chorus again. My own dirty mouth has sung that song. If my tongue could move, it would know how to form the words, though I believe it would refrain from doing so.

My guide's eyes atop his stormy figure were nearly carnal with rage. Foolish human. Of all the half-witted monks you are the most witless, he screamed. No wonder everybody hates you.

That those who were once your friends hate you

that the mightiest people on earth treat you like vermin

that brothers and lay brothers shun you

that the children you taught years ago laughed in your face because they knew you would never dare punish them

that your parents found you useless and disowned you

that even Heinrich left and never returned.

One cannot trust you with the simplest task.

Every lamb in the meadow longed to be slaughtered. The Lord placed them on Æsphydogyllus as sustenance for humans, and it's been centuries since any human set foot here.

Did they not proffer their throats to your blade, displaying every sign of wanton despair? What more could they have possibly offered? Had you requested they rend each other's throats to spare you the stain of blood on your hands, they would have eagerly complied.

Instead, you don't merely murder a son of Æsphydogyllus, the great fish whose back cradled you on Easter night, securing your safety amid boundless waves. No, you slay his firstborn, the sacrosanct crown prince of the entire woeful ocean. A being who bore the title of prince of the gilled youth among the fruits of sorrow, whom all sea monsters had sworn solemn oaths to safeguard, pledging their own claws and teeth to his protection. He who possessed the power to fornicate with every fish species, and whose progeny is duly multifarious. One day he would have grown to be as mighty as his father, who, fortunately, still snores beneath our feet. You have committed an act of regicide and your folly is as deep as the sea.

But time is running out, Othlo, let's go. We must escape before the scent of Æsphydogylli fried offspring reaches his formidable beak or gills, or before he wakes to discover the loss of the apple of his eye, whose body you have just so ineptly dismembered. If we linger on Æsphydogyllus any longer, you will die without a moment to atone for your crime or your sinful life, and your transgressions will drag you down into the deepest abyss of Hell.

How could you think that a human as thoroughly despised as you, so entangled in heinous deeds, could aspire to salvation, when it is written

that even the righteous are barely saved.

In vain I have shown you the heavenly realms and the city. You will never behold them again.

Oh, foolish humans. Oblivious of misery, you casually strip the scales from its fruits and consume their pallid flesh. But you, too, will know misery.

Æwrhul and Teio

The young lay brother firmly clutches Brother Æwrhul's arms, assisting Æwrhul's descent on me, until his blue nose touches my lips. I sense a few of the hairs on the tip of his nose brushing against the tip of my tongue. His arms flail up and down my sides as he hangs suspended, taking in my breath with deep inhalations.

If he has eaten any of those sloes, I can't smell it on him, you can hoist me back up, says Æwrhul. Back on the bed. Check his pulse.

The young lay brother grabs my left arm and squeezes my wrist, though his attention is directed at Æwrhul's timeglass, the gold-encased contraption standing upright on his other palm. A thin stream of sand trickles through it.

He's only a boy, maybe in his fifteenth year now, but tall and broad with a downy blond lip. Enraptured by the wonderful timeglass, he forgets to count my pulse beats and has to turn the glass and start over several times. He squeezes my wrist tightly in excitement.

It's slow, I think. Much slower than the sand, he says and lets go of my arm, which dashes back down alongside the bed. Two fingernails brush the floor, back and forth a few times, then my arm hangs limp.

Slow was my impression, too. Now the urine, Teio. Would you be so kind as to coax it out of him. Remember where to tickle if he retains it.

Near the rod, then behind the stones, like you showed me, says Teio in his nondescript rural dialect.

This trial, too, must stem from sin. This is how I interpret the apparition. Holy Huldarigh. The clumsy fingers underneath the hides, under the robe, fiddling to pull down my braies, bare my sinful parts for further fondling.

Holy Wolfkang.

Emmeram.

Dionysius.

Master, he has already peed a little, says Teio, or it's wet in there at least. Should I put the bowl under him or just taste the wet part of the cowl. We could lick it off, or I could wring some into the bowl, maybe.

O Idolaters

O mancipium stercoris et urinæ

O in sæcularis litteraturæ pompa gloriantes, screamed my guide or companion. So this is the knowledge that the disbelieving brothers of St. Emmeram's monastery rely on before prayer, fast, almsgiving, and penitence. They imbibe their wisdom directly from the chamber pot. To them, the pot is a precious reliquary even, for in the bottom, their teachings are inscribed in very large letters in shit. The only sermon that captures their attention is the grumble of the gut, the pounding blood of ailing bodies, and other such messages, my guide exclaimed in anguish.

Pray for the souls that are blinded and led astray by the shine of temporal teachings. The fumes emanating from their thistle concoctions and herbal salves have gone to their heads. It has made them arrogant and proud like the sorcerers in the court of Pharaoh. They'll remain oblivious to the light that shone over you when your head was immersed in gruel. All their knowledge belongs to the half-perished world where you lie dying, and which itself is withering away, even as you are dying within it. In the true world, the one slowly being pulled down over your heads, their teachings will be worthless. The body and the soul will be one, requiring no other care than the Lord's radiance.

Heaven will shun their company, as the bitter scent from their chamber pot readings clings to them while sweet spices waft from the limbs of true believers, as though their limbs were huge censers blessing every breath taken in the Heavenly Iherusalem. Where the air is heavy with fragrance

while these lost souls stink of long passed, digested things.

Pray for them, Holy Emmeram, Gregors, Wolfkang, and you, too, should pray for them, Brother Othlo. Even as they subject your feeble body to their doctrines, which in the Eternity of Eternities will remain a convoluted system of nonsense, we must pray for them and refrain from reveling in their perdition. Gloating is one of the sinful earthly temptations, and it is certainly not the least of them.

The boy licks his thumb after moistening it in the bowl of liquid painstakingly milked from my cowl.

What does it taste like, Teio. Acidic, sweet, how fungal is it. That's all we need to know, boy, there's no need to dwell on finer details.

Once a year, the City of Heaven celebrates the Feast of Fools. On this day, all those who were haughty followers of temporal doctrines while on earth are summoned from the pits of pain and allowed to deliver lectures in the square. The citizens of Heaven cherish this day. They exchange their radiant white robes for crimson garments, adorning their hair with wildflowers and juicy strawberries, and that in itself, my guide told me, is truly a sight to behold.

The proud scholars are told that their knowledge might earn them heavenly citizenship and deliverance from eternal suffering, provided their lecture convinces the audience of the significance and validity of the worldly arts they dedicated their lives to. As a result, the scholars approach their heavenly lectures with utmost dedication.

As they delve into the taste of urine or the mysteries of the gut, sporting their sullen, proud faces, a few jesters in the crowd cannot resist playing pranks on them as this holiday simply gives them the urge.

A saved soul might be stacking books on top of the scholars' heads while they speak, whispering to them that not a single book can be dropped if they wish to avoid tumbling back into the flamepit.

Another prankster pretends to be an earthly scholar too, redeemed by the Lord because of his lectures in the square. He asks highly detailed questions about the use of herbs named Sillygrass and Gold-Leaved Bumjoy in treating diseases such as Liverfart and Pottythirst, and all the finely dressed citizens are highly amused by the scholars' endeavors to explain, delivering their awkward words through quivering lips as they, in their pride, still cling to the hope that this might secure their redemption.

The laughter on this day is loud and robust. It is the one day of the year when finding delight in the misfortune of others is allowed in Heaven. Usually, the norm there is to mourn for lost souls. However, on this holiday, the saved have no scruples, as the day was conceived by the Lord to amuse them and thus their fun is a way to celebrate Him.

After their lectures, the fools are paraded through the city's wide boulevards in golden carriages decked for celebration. The citizens pelt them with worldly books, amulets, and timeglasses, like the one your wayward flock has purchased at great cost for Brother Æwrhul and his assistants to use in the infirmary.

Finally, a squadron of angels escort them back to the depths and turn them over to their tormentors and slave drivers. However, as they journey back, the angels provide detailed instructions for genuine redemption so that these sinners, too, might find the narrow path from the depths of Hell to life. On rare occasions, a scholar does opt to heed the angels' words rather than succumbing to the terrifying screams and sobs of pain in the realm of shadows. And if he repents and puts his worldly learning behind him, this one might indeed be saved.

Teio wrinkles his nose and presses his round eyes into a squint. It's not at all sweet, he says. I don't know what you mean by fungal. It tastes worse than the other ones.

Hm. Then let me show you how to bloodlet them, I don't have the strength right now. Have you ever slaughtered a pig or a sheep, boy. I need to know if the blood will make you weak.

I can slaughter a hen or cat, says Teio proudly, making it clear that he has no qualms shedding blood.

Can you put on a bandage as well. We'll take it one step at a time.

And you shall know misery, screamed my guide on the back of the great fish Æsphydogyllus, in his fury compressing his body's blue-black airstreams into a storm that made him almost human to behold.

Then I felt the fishback tremble beneath me and I feared the mouth of Hell would yawn open at any moment. In my panic, I sought a place to take cover, finding only the colossal lamb, whom I had playfully dubbed Archipresbyter Werinharius due to his remarkably naive appearance and the slightly deeper, more preachy tone of his bleats compared to the other lambs. I crouched under his belly and clutched the wool of his flanks with both hands.

Spare me, I am a wretched sinner, I didn't know what I did or who I murdered, I cried. It seems probable that this was the moment I wet my robe, although I can't recall with certainty.

The next thing I knew I was airborne. As I was desperately clinging to the giant lamb's belly, my guide had lifted us both and was carrying us through the air to save me from certain death and perdition. Behind us, I saw the great fish Æsphydogyllus shake his back, flinging cliffs, lambs, and trees in all directions so that they whirled around us in our escape.

The smell of his charred son had now reached his gills and in his grief, Æsphydogyllus raised his head from the world sea and let out a scream. Caught between the teeth of his clownishly spotted beak were entire whales and broken church towers, and his scream stirred the waters into a frenzy around him. The waves rose like the gray ramparts of a fortress, then collapsed as though shot down by the catapults of Hell. From every breaking wave, a sea monster showed its face, spewing venomous spray in our direction as we fled.

Common to all sea monsters is their mournful emotional inertia, which is clearly reflected in their appearance. Even their foulest rage appears to humans like a kind of demonstrative lethargy, dressed in fangs, serrations, and tentacles. I have their sluggishness, as monstrous as their immense bodies, to thank for the fact that I am still alive, by the grace of the Lord and His will be done, still breathing the infirmary's polluted air as Teio lets the blood from my arm into the bowl that previously held the liquid from my robe. Listening to the trickle.

It was the fundamental sloppiness of their venomous spraying, a sloppiness stemming from the sea's uniform gray misery, which they are all made of and must spend every hour of their life inside.

As we flew over Oceanus, I also witnessed sea monsters eating each other, and the acts unfolded in a manner that clearly showed both parties' lack of interest in the event.

A horned beast let itself be wrapped in skinny tentacles and dragged toward a triangular slimehead's slowly grinding jaws. Three or more of the translucent arms coiled around the horned creature spontaneously snapped without any apparent effort from the victim, leaving only two tentacles clinging to it, both trembling on the verge of breaking. Even the slightest jerk could have shattered the last chains of snot and the horned creature could have broken free. Yet it allowed itself to be pulled closer to the slimehead and eventually stuffed into its maw where it was ground to a yellowish-chestnut cream in an intricate mill of idly churning teeth. And all this happened without any of the involved even bothering to look at each other. In the sea, to sup and to become supper occur with the same bottomless disinterest.

Each one of these monsters had made a pledge to the king to protect his firstborn. Hence, they were now obliged to display a certain measure of fury and spray their poison in our direction. But they had never promised to act with conviction, in all likelihood lacking the capacity, and so their spume consistently missed its mark.

Only the roar of Æsphydogyllus contained true pain and anger, and in the distance I saw his cliffy body writhe. His tongue extended from his beak, trailing along the clouds, staining their bellies with greenish algae and decay.

Our flight over the furious world sea, with its lethargically raging sea monsters, stretched on for so long that my fear began to wane and I drifted into sleep.

However, by one of God's miracles, my grip on the lamb's flanks never relaxed during my slumber. And thus I was flown across the gray Oceanus, with my guide or companion carrying the lamb which I was holding onto tightly

dreaming peacefully of being back in the scriptorium, arms across the desk, with Heinrich still there, or returned, so that we could continue our whispered conversation about the Trinity and the life of the soul, which was cut short when he left years ago

the last conversation I had with a living person, the last time my voice broke the silence outside of praying or singing the Lord's praises or dictating writings about the mysteries that we could talk about back then

what I long to tell him

and in the dream as in countless dreams before

really told him.

But these bandages are sloppy, not tight enough.

A piece of cloth, already drenched, which the boy tied in haste with a granny knot. Useless peasant. The Lord's will be done.

The blood is already seeping through it, a warm stream down my arm.

Teio hasn't noticed. He's on his way out to dispose of my blood in the infirmary privy and clean the razor. Brother Æwrhul is struggling to rise from the bed, surely lacking the strength himself, as well as the inclination, to spare me one of his sullen glances.

His punishment in Hell for failing to see you bleed and thus allowing you to die, my guide told me, will be to have two chicken rumps for eyes, and through them he will have to squeeze a full basket of spike-covered eggs every day. When he has expelled enough eggs from his bleeding eyebutts to fill a basket, enormous woodlice will hatch from them, and every day this basketful of homegrown produce will proceed to tear and eat his cheeks. Only once a year, on the day of his lecture in the square in Heaven, will he find respite from his labor and his progeny's vicious attacks. But before any of this, it's you who will bleed to death, Othlo, and you who will reckon with your Maker. By the Lord's divine plan, it shall come to pass, with three angels watching over your bedside.

So far from a spear or a rusty blade in the belly, so spoiled even in death. The stomachache is almost gone, and even at its highest, it was bearable.

Hence the thought

that this bloodletting might have actually worked

the Lord's will through bloodletting actually worked

But the Lord's will was not for the bloodletting to work, only that I should lie here

dying

with this feeling that

if the bloodletting weren't going to kill me

which it will

by the Lord's design

it might have actually worked

by the Lord's design. He works in mysterious ways.

One wipes the sweat off my forehead, one mitigates the air with incense and wingbeats, one sits ready to write an intercession if I believe and repent deeply enough. But if I believed and repented deeply enough I would be able to see them and sense their assistance.

The Lord will not let his angels tighten those bandages. My blood would stain their radiant robes. Their fingers are made of starshine, unsuited to tighten granny knots on bloody earthly swathes.

Soon the bells will announce the upcoming mass. Æwrhul and Teio will leave the infirmary, and if survival is too much to hope for, then one can hope to bleed out in near silence.

The comfort of the lamb

The City of Heaven is silent and light

while the City of Hell

Antiherusalem

is always busy and dark.

There are no homes in this city and no rest. Only workshops, forges, ergastula, slaughterhouses, depots, sweatshops, quarries, archives, tanneries, smelting halls, brothels, field kitchens, cranes, mills, and scaffolds. But nothing is permanent. It is a big construction site in perpetual reconstruction following the infernal builder's smudged schematics

yesterday's brothel is today's library

the constant labor is carried out in the dark. Cathedrals must be built to honor the great adversary. But since nothing is constant here apart from darkness and labor, the cathedrals are torn down again as soon as they are raised, their great stones crushed to render them useless for other purposes. Monks are harnessed like animals to carts loaded with stones. Unless their sins qualify them for something worse.

Any labor that humans have endured to earn their bread through the sweat of their brows, you will find again in the City of Hell. Baking, weaving, fulling, grinding, whoring, hammering, brewing, sowing, plowing, harvesting, and hunting while being tortured. For a sinful soul who has not learned to despise the world, Hell will seem familiar and somewhat homely. This is why, in spite of their suffering, they are unable to locate the narrow path to Life and perhaps are not even trying to. In Hell, they still have their desires, and though their satisfaction is seldom allowed, the sinner feels safer being ruled by desires than liberated from them. They can't undo the hooks and ties from their throats and scrotums for they have been led by them their entire lives, convinced that the pull represents their own volition.

The ocean was no longer under us. We flew in a darkness that seemed endless, but we had rearranged ourselves so that I was now riding on Archipresbyter Werinharius with my guide or companion below us, carrying the lamb on his whirlstorm back.

The darkness was so dense, it blinded me and I had to close my eyes and hide them behind my hands. But some of this deeper darkness still penetrated my hands and eyelids.

Unlike the earthly darkness, which we understand to be a mere absence of light, the Erebus darkness is actively streaming, radiant, and as we flew, there was no flicker of the cleansing flames to break it as Hell City was still far away.

But from the dark I heard screams, coming from all directions, men, women, and wailing infants who had died before receiving baptism. Some screams were distant, others quite close. We sped past them, and it occurred to me that our trajectory was likely downward, that the screams around us must be from the falling, and that, thanks to my guide's powers, we were descending much faster toward the pits of Hell than the poor souls alongside us.

I will reveal to you Hell beyond your own time, just as I have shown you Heaven after Judgment Day. For as long as there are people on Earth, the streets of both Iherusalem and Antiherusalem remain empty, waiting to be populated, and this sight would not have been nearly as educational for you to witness, nor as enjoyable for me to show you.

While you were sleeping, lost in pitiful dreams of the friend who left you, we crossed Oceanus and came to the land of Necubia. Here, the people are neither very virtuous nor very wicked, tedium and mild humdrum reign. Since your heavy eyelids refused to remain open when I attempted to unveil this marvel, we shall have to revisit it once we have seen Hell, said my guide with a strained sigh. In the heart of the land of Necubia, the great Dragon raises its head and I will let you peek into its foul mouth and eyes. We ventured into its mouth willingly and are presently descending down its throat to Antiherusalem. However, the sinful souls are ushered there by angels, and none shall reach the depths where true torments begin until the first angel of the Revelation has pursed his lips around his trumpet, heralding the hour of Judgment.

In that moment, Cain, the first of the doomed, overgrown with moss and vines during his millennia-spanning descent, will knock his head into the gleaming cobbles of Hell's square and Antiherusalem will have its very first citizen. A few days later, he will be joined by his sister Awan, his own flesh and blood, because he knew her as a woman and begat children by her.

I will show you Hell City, teeming as it will be after Judgment Day, but first let me tell you, and mark my words, that while your worldly body is still gushing blood onto the floor of Saint Emmeram's infirmary with no one noticing and the Lord allowing it, for it is His will, Cain has long spotted the fiery city below, and its heat is already searing his brows and lashes, despite no one but the Lord knowing the hour of Judgment

not before the trumpet sounds and Cain's green forehead splits open on Hell's cobbles. After falling for millenia in this darkness, the crack of his skull will be a cool and welcome sensation, nothing compared to what lies ahead.

The stream of darkness seemed to ease a little, I was able to open my eyes and discover the cleaved towers and barracks of the city below. We landed in a deserted square surrounded by black toothstump towers. The towers shone with an inner glow, a shared light pulsating within them. The square was empty but from every direction distant screams could be heard.

At this point, my guide or companion told me something about this square being constructed to receive nobilities and dignitaries among the damned, but I failed to pay attention to this part of his narrative.

For the moment we landed, as I slid down the lamb's back, I saw that the lamb had been gravely wounded, indeed its right hind leg was entirely missing and it was now limping pitifully on its three legs on the cobblestones with a blackened, frothing stump of the missing leg twitching behind it. I realized that the lamb must have been struck by a drop of the sea monsters' venomous spray, and that this drop had devoured its leg.

I looped my arms around Archipresbyteris Werinharii neck, pressed my face into the wool, and wept. I wept and cried for the brave lamb who had served as my shelter and only salvation on the back of Æsphydogyllus, and who for my sake had lost his green island home in the miserable gray ocean, lost his brothers and sisters and entire family and now his leg, too, and who, even in the face of severe exhaustion, pain, and peril, had never emitted anything but the most good-natured bleating

and it was with this mournful yet loving sound that Archipresbyter Werinharius now met my guilt-laden embrace. I stroked his nose and patted his flanks and did my best to convey the profound regret I felt for the losses he had suffered and the pain I alone, with my misdeed, had inflicted, which had now brought him all the way to the pits of Hell, lonely, legless, and with no hope of future frolicking.

We stood like that for a long time, me with my arms around his neck and he with his head on my shoulder, entwined in grief and apprehension but also genuine joy to still be alive and on this journey together. And for this reason, I promised Archipresbyter Werinharius that I would do anything in my power to bring him back from Hell's abyss and find him a new home.

A hill with lush grass and other lambs for company. And though your wound, your terrible loss, the memory of venomous demons, and most recently the blinding darkness you have had to endure will mark you from the other lambs, make your heart heavier and your gaze less innocent, there is still a chance of a tolerable life.

Thus I spoke to Archipresbyter Werinharius with my hands buried deeply in his soft fleece, and he bleated in response, whatever it meant.

Oh, you most witless among half-witted monk-men, my guide or companion cried, beating my shoulder with a whirlwind so I could feel the cold blowing through my cowl and tunic.

It must be noted that neither the lamb nor I sensed the hellflames, which include both warm and cold varieties. This, too, had been explained to me by my guide as we hurtled toward the square. It is the nature of these flames to punish and cleanse the damned, but since we were alive and not damned, these flames were not permitted to burn or freeze us. Therefore, Hell appeared to have a tolerable climate, considerably more hospitable than our monastery during winter, when the delicate brothers wrap their bodies in furs and wool where the eyes can't see, yet still lament the cold on their way to Mass, completely disregarding the summum silentium that the Holy Benedictus has imposed on us.

But when my guide struck me, I felt the cold boring deep into my shoulder and exclaimed, surprised and hurt, wait no.

I have been tasked to show you Heaven and Hell and all the Lord's marvels in between. It is your, I think, rather modest duty to stay alert so you can tell others of what you have seen when you return to your earthly life, for as it is written

what I say to you, I say to everyone.

But as if it weren't enough that you, in your bloated carnality, failed to keep your eyes open as we passed over Necubia, now you're wasting your brief visit in Hell, too, idly petting some soulless piece of livestock that you ought to have slaughtered, a creature who, since it first laid eyes on you, has pleaded for you to cut its throat.

Othlo, I cannot stress this enough, if you don't heed what I show and tell you now, you will be reacquainted with Hell in the most intimate of fashions.

We crossed the square, pieces of broken skull scattered all around, crunching beneath my sandals and the giant lamb's remaining hooves, this being the abrupt end point for all damned souls.

We did see a few falls concluding in this manner, with the damned heads shattering against the cobbles, and I was told that these damned belonged to my own time, more or less, and that I had to watch out to avoid being struck by a recent sinner.

We passed down rows of black toothstump towers, and even the towers looked damned and tortured. On each tower was a pair of brown eyes, which looked much like the eyes of a dog after it has been scolded by its owner for biting a child, and with these eyes the towers watched us, tears welling up in the corners and breaking like waves, sounding as they hit the ground like someone tuning a mighty bell by chiseling its underside. These were the bell towers of Antiherusalem, and the tolling, their weeping, was announcing the arrival of a new citizen to the angels of Hell.

Behind the towers was the actual city. Here, the land and air burn. Between the flamepits and flameditches are swarming flames, burning from invisible torches, so that all enter the city under its veil of fire. The little airborne flames are of both the hot and cold variety, and since it is impossible to tell them apart, one never knows which of the two pains to expect next.

The flames are so numerous that at least one is inhaled in every breath, torturing the body from within by frying or freezing the throat and lungs, while countless other flames perpetually lash at the citizen's bare skin

and it is worth noting that almost all Antiherusalemites are naked as a punishment for their shamelessness on Earth, and perhaps to keep their sinful lust alive, as the slave-driving angels and magistrates of Hell prefer not to give up their prey.

The swarming flames in the air are the least of the citizens' sufferings, but they're also the only ones that remain constant, the rest being as changing as they are ingenious, which is why the Antiherusalemites have dubbed them the flames of mercy and often try to inhale as many as they can, holding their breath during particularly agonizing moments, striving to contain the pain within them until it can't intensify any further

as it is a widespread belief among them, true or not, that a human can only be apportioned so much pain before they are cleansed and ready to win citizenship in the City of Heaven, and almost all the damned prefer the predictable pain from the flames of mercy over the highly unpredictable agony they might otherwise suffer at the hands of the punishing angels and their various instruments of torture.

For the most part, humans are punished with inspiration drawn from their own imagination. In Hell, the tools are set free from their maker's hand, and humans are punished for imitating God in their crafting of tools, no matter how vital these tools may have seemed for their survival.

Hell is skill and craftsmanship and the damned are both the craftsmen and their materials. The tools, however, have a master will and a master power of their own. They are only partly commanded by tormentors, slave drivers, and builders and might suddenly revolt against them. In Hell, the tools are set free from maker, owner, and purpose alike.

The fact that human tools have such an essential role in the torments of Hell suggests, for someone who knows how to read the apparition, that suffering itself is instrumental in nature, that all kinds of agony, in Hell as on Earth, function as tools under the control of a higher power, a power who knows how to wield them and always has a specific purpose in selecting a particular type of suffering to be employed against us

to knead us

puff us up

chop us down into the intended shape

every bit of pain and misery is a tool meticulously designed to fulfill its own specific function

every bit of pain and misery is merely a tool

and every tool we invent

to earn our bread through the sweat from our brows

will be turned against us and used to torture the mortals and the damned on Earth and in Hell.

This is the plight of human creativity, that every bright idea will immediately become a torture instrument in a higher power's hand, as it often already is in our own. Our foreheads shall be held to the grinding stone, the spoon from which we merrily slurped shall scoop our eyes from their sockets and our Adam's apples from our throats.

They rounded up the children in a line by the church wall. Two knights led the way, swinging their swords at the children's ankles, followed by two others thrusting long spears into the fallen. The weather was frosty, a thick mist flowed from the children's wounds and screaming mouths, but that did not spare me from the sight.

I lay on the cart, barely visible on a cushion of cloth bags, my scrawny body wrapped in blankets and weighed down under my father's bearskin. Only my head peeked out, elevated just enough for me to witness the slaughter my father had ordered.

And what struck me the most was not the sight of blood and

guts, but how unattractive these children, roughly my own age, appeared. Even their death rattle did little to offset their hideousness, the last screams and final words in their ugly language merely irritated me under my bearskin. Or so I realized later.

All of it, all the suffering in Hell and on Earth, has purpose and meaning.

No matter how awful we are, we do rid the world of ourselves step-by-step, and the Lord rids the silence and empty space of the world. Only a few, the very best of us, remain in the heavenly Iherusalem, as minuscule as a bubble from the world sea or a particle of crust from the massifs. And this tiny bit of good is siphoned off from the damned.

Of all the suffering I witnessed in Hell City, only the lamb's was entirely pointless. Thus, it was only for the soulless lamb that my tears continued to flow.

The ditch, the pigsty, and the brothel

We stopped by a ditch full of emaciated sinners. The surface was lit by the airborne flames, but the way the bodies writhed and switched places with new arrivals gave the impression that this was only the top layer of a much deeper cavern. The impression was enhanced by the noise from the growling stomachs of each, which drowned out their own screams and the screams of all around them.

Here the damned did not partake in the infernal construction nor any of Hell's other work. The extent of their sentence was to lie in the pit and writhe in hunger.

My guide told me that they had been the most gluttonous richfolk once, and now they were tormented by hunger and thirst. They had to take turns ripping the teeth out of their own gums and pulling the nails off their fingers to use as currency, merely to buy the privilege of sucking on a few bites of indigestible rotten crabmeat.

The ones in the top layer were considered the poorest since the crabmeat was at the bottom. The rich were the few who had stolen, traded, or charmed their way into possessing the most nails and teeth, and they only allowed the crabmeat to circulate between each other's suckling gums, while those closer to the top had little prospect of ever obtaining a claw or a piece of shield and had been swindled out of whatever currency they might have had to begin with.

Was it worth the pain, I shouted against the noise of the thousand grumbling stomachs

were your pleasures worth this, you miserable creatures

but they may not have heard me. Their eyes were set on my mouth and remaining teeth, which they hoped to wrest from me with their usurious offers, so that I might soon, in exchange for my teeth, be feasting royally on crabmeat along with them at the bottom

where chests brimming with nails and teeth awaited me

and for only a fraction of this, my future wealth, they offered to extract my teeth and nails quickly and painlessly, sparing me the ordeal. Others, more modest, offered to assess the value on my teeth in exchange for a small fee. Still others merely pleaded for me to urinate into their thirsty mouths.

Were your pleasures worth all this, I shouted, then turned away from the ditch of gluttons.

Before the great brothel lay the Jews' pigsty.

Sows bulging with lard and bigger than oxen, why even bigger than Archipresbyter Werinharius, staggered around in the mud, each weighed down by at least a dozen men sucking milk from their teats, eating excrement, and taking turns to try to fornicate with them, constantly fighting over whose turn it was.

The very sight of the sows made the men horny. However, they were not allowed to fulfill their urges nor were they even capable, although from time to time they did manage to wriggle their erections into the rear end of a reluctant sow.

In the middle of the Jews' pigsty, their elders were seated, each clutching a scroll of parchment in one hand and a fistful of pig shit in the other, fingering the latter while interpreting and discussing their infidel scrolls. Their long beards were stiff and spiky with shit, which appeared to be a sign of dignity.

Evidently, they considered the sows to be particularly enlightened scribes, because whenever a dispute over a passage arose among them, they tried to enlist a sow to interpret it and then were left to decipher the meaning of the sow's uninterested grunt. This only prolonged their debates.

Were your sins worth it, I screamed

and those not preoccupied with suckling the sows' teats or trying to enter them from behind hushed me with their shitmouths as it was imperative not to interrupt the council of elders perusing the scrolls.

Only one of the scribes emerged from the mud and screamed back at me. He was a vain one with big, bushy brows that he seemed quite proud of as he had managed to keep them clean and white in the middle of his shit-encrusted face.

You can't judge like that, he screamed back, by what right do you assume our existence to be intolerable. And even if it were, then by what right do you assume that this suffering is a punishment rather than simply the terms of the existence. He continued to hurl such nonsense at me along with fistfuls of mud and feces from the sows, none reached me, however, as it was eagerly intercepted and eaten by other members of his infidel bloodline long before it posed a threat to my spotless robe.

I scoffed at the obstinate fellow and turned away from the Jews.

We wandered through the corridors of the large brothel, where all the angels divinely appointed as slave drivers and executioners in Hell are permitted to satiate their urges with the damned. The fallen angels, on the other hand, banished from Heaven, are denied entry to the brothel and can only whore among each other.

With utmost dignity, the Lord's angels move through these enormous barracks, displaying no hint of shame or base desires. The lust that they by the Lord's design are capable of rousing in their genitals is not connected to their hearts, and when they drive their sex into the damned, they do so with a sedate smile of innocence, radiating pure devotion to the Lord. This elevated look never falters, never descends to anything less divine.

They will wear the same drowsy, innocent gaze when they swing their swords at the final generation.

The offspring of sinners and angels fluttered through the brothel's corridors, winged genitals of both species, some with badgers' claws at the tip or venom-dripping mandibles along the lips. I constantly had to brush these bugs off my face as they tried to eat or enter it.

A third type of offspring seemed less appalling. They were rectums with mottled butterfly wings, adorned with myriad patterns and of unusual color splendor. They flitted peacefully around, farting in the already heavy brothel air, but that was the extent of their aggression.

They are called the tonsures of Hell, my guide told me, and they are pulled down over the heads of stupid monks like me as soon as we step under Antiherusalem's veil of fire to begin serving our sentence.

In the booths flanking the labyrinthine corridors, I saw adulterers and lechers suffer in the arms of violent angels. So violent, in fact, that the down from their wings fell like snow through the air, settling on the floors of both booths and corridors. As it mingled with the blood and shimmering angel semen already pooled on the ground, a sludge was created that made every step treacherous. I stumbled repeatedly, and poor Archipresbyter Werinharius skidded hopelessly around on his three remaining hooves.

No type of embrace was out of bounds for the angels to perform, and consequently, the sinners who suffered them were constantly in a state of pregnancy or birthing. While an angel was engaged one way, the damned playmate was often simultaneously giving birth to winged monstrosities through one or two other orifices.

If every orifice was already occupied by an angel, the offspring, using claws or mandibles, would bore a new pathway out, and this hole could then be used for further impregnation, meaning that each whore in Hell could accommodate up to eight angels at a time while giving birth to three monsters

and if the situation should arise that every available entrance was being used as an exit, the angels would bore new entrances, using the torture instruments ever at hand near the beds.

Miserable people, I screamed at these too, meretrices et adulteri, were your pleasures worth this

but my guide or companion hushed me, reminding me that I might easily end up in these surroundings, which was the very reason he was showing me the brothel

and he also reminded me that no matter how busy and bustling the place appeared, there would always be an available booth and a shameful bed for anyone deserving of it.

Light, hoarse, and exhausted wailing from the next bed down. That must be Gehrwas. It is still day, or another day, a square of blue sky high above, not belonging, not entirely at least, to the half-perished world where we lie dying, this light of the true world shining down on ours.

It's four or five days ago, and it was quite runny. Runnier than normal. But now it feels more like a lump, a tight feeling right here, Holy Emmeram, stand by me, no, below the belly, there, please don't touch it, don't touch me there.

And it's arrogant Æwrhul himself leaning over the sickbed and judging by the wails erupting, he is pressing the tender spot firmly, despite the pleas not to. He says that the belly is a pot for cooking food, and that Gehrwas must have neglected to provide his belly with the proper fuel to bring the content to a boil, causing it to spill something raw and uncooked into his guts.

He ought to give a lecture on that at the Feast of Fools.

Were your pleasures worth this, Gehrwas

the pleasure you hoped to experience as you dragged yourself to the privy at night with your lame leg like a deadweight trailing after you, even before the need to go became pressing.

This punishment, too, is meaningful, and the Lord is only retaining your waste to prevent you from sinfully enjoying its disposal. You should be thanking the Lord for your condition instead of seeking Brother Æwrhul's assistance in the infirmary.

But had I been able to speak now

Deo permittente

I doubt I would have broken my silence to say it.

As I was screaming at the sinners who were receiving their rightful punishments in the booths of the brothel, I must admit I felt more fear than anger. A sinful desire very close to my nature had seized me, and my flesh betrayed my faith by showing itself willing to whore here, in the midst of the infernal torments and humiliations, with the very punishment displayed before my eyes. Indeed, it was the punishment itself tempting the flesh.

Everywhere I looked, I saw fluttering body parts, the very kind that I in my youth had paid good money to behold in chambers, gazing for quite a while before lustfully throwing myself at them and letting myself be immersed

and before I knew it, I'd slipped on the floor and a throng of winged beasts had swooped down on me, lifting my robe with their claws and mandibles to expose my shameful readiness.

A small, winged pudendal beast of the genus feminine with curly-red-haired spider legs along its side squeezed itself around my readiness, working it eagerly by jumping up and down on its many-jointed legs while tightening its lips around me and alternately threatening and caressing me with its mandibles.

Since the she-beast's crooked feet, which formed the basis of its leaps, had immediately penetrated the skin of my belly and thighs, I couldn't rip it out without inflicting great damage on myself. But this was not the only reason I hesitated to remove it.

Holy Emmeram.

The isolated nature of this body part, the fact that there was no body attached to it, created the feeling that it belonged to every woman I had ever sinfully wanted in my life and never had

it was like seeing a thousand spectral women around this beast, completing the beast, containing it like their ghost-flesh-hidden secret

that this she-beast was in fact the shame-canal between the ghost-thighs of every desired woman ever all the women I had dreamed of since becoming a man, all the women who have driven me to forget my work in the scriptorium, where I could copy or dictate and seek oblivion and boredom

to avoid the sight of the streets

avoid pulling a cart between the beauties

never again wash a foot, the rounded heel, the arched ankle

produce eight flawless copies of Saint Wolfkang's life

remember Heinrich's words

a dialogue about the life course of the soul, and another about the Holy Trinity, Heinrich's words and mine, whispered inside the scriptorium

later copied in silence or dictated listlessly

I have not spoken to anyone since, never

what I long to say to him

using my voice only for opus Dei, praising the Lord and dictating the words we once spoke in the scriptorium, writing down the dialogues, then never speaking again

through the summum silentium of the half-perished world, the Lord's choir sings, through the Lord's choir, the silentium cæleste can be heard.

The pudendal beast exuded fluids and emitted every kind of sigh I had ever secretly dreamed of hearing. The mandibles caressed my readiness with jumps and squeezes. Yet the tenderness of her venom-dripping jaws carried an unmistakable threat.

I wasn't able to free myself of this sinful pleasure without inflicting considerable damage. I should never have hesitated, but I did fear it and I did hesitate. Holy Huldarigh.

The green eyes above mine

then the brown eyes

the blue-gray

the tip of her tongue brushing the upper lip

her eyes rolling back in voluptatibus carnis

her own hand clutching her small breast

now the breasts are large and bouncing and her eyes demanding

now a downy blond upper lip

a line of blond curls reaching her navel

a pale scar across a dirt-gray face

now squinting, blind eyes

beautiful, light-brown eyes, merely for decoration

despite squinting to see the half-perished world where we lie dying

her black curls falling on my face

we were shrouded in darkness now

then the darkness lifted from my eyes at last and all the joy drained from my shame.

My guide or companion had snatched the pudendal beast, and it had willingly unhooked its myriad legs from the skin of my thighs and belly, its sharp mandibles releasing my readiness without a struggle

willingly ending our embrace

as though to spare me

and my guide was tearing at her, pulling at the edges of her lips with his clenched airstreams until she ripped apart and fell to the ground, dead, in two convulsing pieces.

In my blunt misery I turned to her torn remains and kissed her salty flesh goodbye as my guide thundered over me, declaring my soul lost and dead for all Eternity of Eternities to the Lord and our Savior Ihesus Christ

whose death on the cross would have been entirely in vain if all souls were as sinful as mine.

The tapestry of entrails

Exhausted and grieving, I was thrown over the back of Archipresbyter Werinharius by my guide, who wanted no more delays whatsoever. Limping on its three legs, the lamb carried me out of the brothel and down the senseless alleys of Antiherusalem, my guide walking in front, stormy because of my sinfulness.

Certain of my perdition, I gently caressed the lamb's large head and whispered soothing words into its ears. There is still hope for you, I said. I can't avoid returning here for my cleansing punishments, but I was promised that after this brief visit in Hell, I'd be shown the land of Necubia, and if I don't live to take you somewhere better, then at least I will take you to Necubia, the land of indifferent and barely tolerable things.

For a lamb who has witnessed the pain and darkness of Hell and faced immense losses and suffering, the barely tolerable might even be preferable to outright happiness. The grassy slopes with the frolicking lambs are unlikely to be found there. But excessive happiness might feel blinding to the grief-stricken, and one who has known pain won't yearn for happiness afterward. Only the souls who have been allowed to quench their thirst in the river of oblivion can bear to meet happiness after the torments.

In the land of Necubia we may find a slope somewhat less lovely than what I previously promised. The grass is probably brownish there with the occasional thistle and shrubs of bitter rue. But surely edible for someone with modest demands, and besides, the other lambs will understand your thousand-year bleakness. No one will be frolicking in the meadows, more like trudging heavily through withered things. But all the withered plants will be yours and your trudging will be shared.

Now we traversed the alleys which were home to the infernal workshops. Tanners and fellmongers skinned each other, carefully scraping and cleaning the skins using their teeth under the strict supervision of the punishing angels, while cooks took turns making broth from each other to feed the Lord's slave drivers.

But the biggest and worst of all the infernal districts is the weavers' square. Here, the entrails of the damned are woven into a large tapestry. Along the edges of a frame the size of ten cathedrals hung thousands of the damned with their bellies ripped open. A team of master weavers in dented armor flew around on carrion birds' backs, carrying the twisted entrails in their hands, threading the weft through the warp. From time to time, a bird couldn't resist throwing off its rider to peck a hole in the tapestry, thus ensuring that the magnificent work could never be finished as it also served as food for crows and jackdaws.

As we rode past it, I couldn't divert my eyes from the horrible tapestry. It pictured all the wrongs of the world and the sins of the damned, and in the center was a portrait of the great opponent himself, complete with his melting steel beak and goat horns, as he is a vain ruler desiring recognition through all the labor done in Hell.

In a corner of the tapestry, I saw myself sitting in the scriptorium, fat-bellied and with my carnal lust peeking through my robe. Torpidly I sat, my mouth open, drops of gall depicting my five remaining teeth-stumps, writing my book about my own temptations.

On the top of the page I sat bent over, it said

> There was once a learned man who took pleasure in many types of sin, but as the Lord had frequently cautioned him to change his ways, he turned himself around and became a monk without anyone close to him knowing. In the place where he became a monk, he met many people of varied natures, some who read worldly books and others who read the holy scriptures, and he started exclusively emulating those who devoted themselves to lectio divina. However, the more he read, the more he felt the spark of a devilish temptation spreading within.

So masterful is the tapestry of entrails, I recognized every flourish of my handwriting, which is easily recognizable as I taught myself how to write as a child, long before receiving any proper guidance, which is also why I have never learned to hold the quill correctly. Even in the smallest particulars, I found the tapestry's representation of my writing to be impeccable.

Mesmerized, I gazed at that page in the book of my temptations, the tiny woven letters so confusingly similar to mine

until I realized that these letters in the tapestry must have been created using the intestines of the crying infants nailed to the frame between grown men and women and in that very moment I decided never to let my hand write another word, not even if the abbot or my guide commanded me to, lest these words be woven with the guts of unbaptized children in Hell. I heard their pitiful wailing every time the weft was tightened or a master weaver pulled at the intestine, and I heard men and women who, at the height of their pain, managed to stifle their screams to sing to the little torn ones, speaking to them with tenderness, like a mother or a father would

and the sound weighed heavily on my heart, even though I knew that the children were impure in the Lord's eyes.

Certain of my perdition, furious with my guide for having taken me here, and still grieving the she-beast he had killed in the brothel

as the carnal joy she had granted me was bigger than anything I had experienced on earth

I leaned against the giant lamb's head and whispered in his ear

that this journey, for which I had regretfully dragged him along, had been arranged solely for me to learn from the apparitions I was shown in Heaven and Hell

but that I no longer wished to draw any lessons from it.

That I no longer wished for anyone to become wiser through such torments, and that any lesson involving even the most distant memory of Hell was undesirable, and that from this moment until my return as one of the damned, I longed only for oblivion, however brief and as my perdition was nonnegotiable anyway, I now intended to seek the earthly oblivion with determination, boozing, whoring, and eating bloody food with the other miserable existences.

Considerable amounts of vomit welled from my throat, interspersing my whispered words, even if I had not eaten since our visit in Heaven, when I roused my guide's ire by nibbling on the smallest of the gold onions. The lamb, too, was throwing up as he limped past the tapestry, overpowered by the stench of excrement from the ripped and stretched intestines suspended above us.

Also in the tapestry, I saw Heinrich leaving our monastery, happy and carefree, riding a donkey through the gates. My own figure could be seen in the background, stooping with my sex erect, drops of rectal secretions trembling in the corners of my eyes to illustrate my grief at parting with the wisest, most loving man I have ever known.

HENRYGUS
GYROVAGUS
SARABAITA

read the sign around the donkey's neck, and through my vomiting, I shook with anger over these insults, which must have been woven into the tapestry solely to mock me.

I saw Gehrwas dragging his dead leg toward the privy, hoping to enjoy a moment's defecation, and I saw Æwrhul buying his timeglass for a pouch full of money while the poor starved and froze in the streets of Recanespurch.

In dark cellars I saw the flesh outgrowing its shackles, and in the woods of ancient idols I saw Christian limbs dangling from the trees. The severed head of the holy Dionysius peeked above the rosy walls of the heavenly palace and he flinched.

Long-bearded brothers and shaved laymen. Women with intricately braided hair in church, cheeks painted thickly and frivolously. Fratricide, patricide, depraved embraces.

I saw eight children, lined up against the clay wall of a squalid church, sword blades cutting through the air and hitting their ankles, the spear-bearers behind them ready to finish them off. There was no one living left in the town to mourn them or pray for them.

My father on horseback, armored, pointing at the children and giving the order

and myself on the cart under his bearskin, with my small eyes full of contempt and impatience.

Even at this distance and through the frosty air, I sensed the stench from the children's torn bowels. Thus I had a waft of the hellish tapestry even as a child, though fifty years would pass before I saw it suspended above me in all its horror.

I would have covered my eyes, even more, I would have ripped my eyes out along with my nose and shoved them down my own throat if that could have spared me the sight and the stench, but I could not. It was not my guide stopping me, but another force, something perhaps not even belonging to the outside world, that held my eyes fixed on the tapestry.

We try to love you anyway

Brother Othlo, says someone, says Gehrwas on the bed next to mine. If you're awake, Brother.

His words are mixed with crying, tainting what we have of summum silentium in the cold infirmary, the cold that I now truly feel. It's so dark now, I can't distinguish the darkness of the starless sky from that of the infirmary or the darkness behind my eyelids

but the outside darkness is free of snoring, grunting, or constipated cripples crying

hence the need to differentiate, as it would enable me to determine which darkness to direct my longing at.

If you're awake, Brother Othlo, I must speak to you. I know you're going to live and I'm going to die now. I've seen you turn lame and lie stiff and deathlike three times before or more. Then the boils will erupt on your body and you will walk again. You will rise from your bed like you've done before and resume your responsibilities. You will serve the Lord with renewed zeal, even more austere and irritable than before.

But I've dreamed, and it was Saint Wolfkang himself. He spoke to me, to the clubfoot. Can you imagine. He told me that you're going to live, Brother Othlo, and he said that you wouldn't be very pleased about it. And then he pointed at me, indicating the location of the pain. You won't get rid of that one, he said.

Pray for me if you can hear me, Brother Othlo. Pray in your heart if you can't move your lips, for the Holy Wolfkang pointed at me and said, you won't get rid of that one, my son

he pressed my stomach, here, where the pain burns the worst, he pressed his blessed

and you, who hate and despise, not just the world but all of us. You will be allowed to rise from your sickbed.

We are here to love God

Lord, my life and my hope are at your mercy now

but we are also here to love our next of kin, don't forget Benedicti words, which you once shared with me, and don't forget Ihesu own words

because you hate, Brother Othlo, I could always tell.

But we try to love you anyway. Please remember that before you wake up with renewed austerity. Let my words carry the gravity of approaching death. Every brother in the monastery is here to love. They're not as smart as you so you must forgive and you must love them. And don't forget that it was the clubfoot Gehrwas whom Saint Wolfkang spoke to.

He was radiant but otherwise foul like me. His beard was long and he was dressed in rags, like the hermit he wanted to be and not the bishop he was made to be. And he stank, Brother Othlo, like the rotten bog he wished to live in.

You wouldn't have cared for him, even if you wrote an entire book about him. I don't think you would have cared to see him. But maybe he knew that since he chose to speak to someone else.

Who's speaking, who's awake, we're permitted to speak. Are you in need of comfort, Brother.

No. It's the pain. Forgive me for waking you. It won't happen again. May the Lord watch over you in your sleep.

Yes, we're all in pain here. Is that you with the sloes on your stomach. Then you did it to yourself. That's a terrible thing to eat. They tighten up your mouth like a bishop's asshole, that's what my father used to say. Was that what you were saying about bishops. And the moment they get inside your tummy, that's when the trouble starts. You should really avoid eating them altogether, that's my opinion.

But you've had no meals since you came. I keep a check on that because no one else does. Æwrhul is too busy. I even tried telling the staff who bring the food. Several times. While you were sleeping.

The day before yesterday I had nothing to eat either. You know why. Because I asked if there was onion in the sausages. There you go. I can't tolerate those chunky onion pieces anymore, they give me fluctuations and then my tummy overflows. You all would've had the brunt, farts and thunder all night, how'd you like that. You have to be careful what you expose your stomach to, especially as you get older. Personally, I wouldn't have touched those sloes with a pole.

But they tossed my sausages to the dogs and I was offered nothing instead, such as fish or something cured. How d'you like that. So I had nothing to eat before gruel. Are you awake. We can talk, it's our prerogative in the infirmary. The Lord demands no silence from the sick or the old, as a small consolation in our suffering. The Lord is fairly good to us. We're allowed to protest when we're treated unfairly, and even if no one listens, it's comforting to say it out loud.

I've been silent for decades, but now I'm allowed to speak. Listen. The other night I was saying that I wished the dogs would shit in his mouth, in the mouth of the one who took my sausages without giving me fish or something cured instead, and that I hoped the dogs had stomach cramps from the onions before shitting. Holy Emmeram preserve me, I really said that. Are you listening. I've been silent like the grave since your mother sucked teat, long before she grew teats of her own. I'm done with silence.

Words of no importance billow in the heavy air, and as each word is spoken, another lies in wait, mindless, intangible, ceaseless

much lighter than the infirmary air and as steady as the stream of Tonach, whose rushing they drown out as shifting as our pain and grief and as steadily flowing, as futile as everything else that points only toward its own end

words wrung out of life, yet lifeless on their own

like the tonsures of Hell, little assholes with butterfly wings

however splendid the colors and patterns on their wings, the rotten stench from their intangible insides remains the same

we only have words for impermanence and falsehoods

no word for the light I saw, shining from the clouds and the light I saw through the gruel

only through the earthly silence, the heavenly praise can be heard, and louder than the heavenly praise is the heavenly silence.

Under the scourge

No punishment in Antiherusalem surpasses the great adversary's, just as no crime on earth surpasses his crime against the Lord.

He is chained to his seat, a glowing grate over the flamepit where the hot and cold flames of mercy originate. Tall flames, both hot and cold, blow around his hunched mightiness. He writhes on the grate to alternate which parts of him are freezing or burning or to catch a prey, which he eats and then shits into the pit.

Using the steel claws at the end of his wing, which is always either frozen or aflame, he snatches anything within reach, human or angel, rips it open and shoves it down one of his colossal steel beaks, either the one at the center of his furious head or the one located in the sinister face on his rear.

Around this steel-beaked, two-headed goat-bird who seems to encompass all the torments of Hell are the smithies of Antiherusalem, a cleaved wasp's nest pulsing with light.

In the middle of every cell, a hellsmith is shaping the red-hot steel, using his bare hands as the hammer and the back of another hellsmith as the anvil. They must continually forge new claws and chains for the great adversary, as everything placed over the flamepit promptly melts.

Small groups of monks cart the claws for the tips of Satan's wings and it's their task to fasten them, but only few manage to do so without getting caught and eaten, that is unless he simply flings them into the pit, or they tumble through the openings in the grate by themselves. Others are tasked with changing the sharp beaks and still others must switch out the chains to ensure he will never rise from his sentence. Entire battalions of carts carrying claws, beaks, and chains are wheeled in from all directions under the fiery angelic flogging. If his beak and claws liquify entirely before they are replaced, he uses his goat horns to ram, as his horns are impervious to melting although white with heat.

Surrounding him on the grate are whores and sorceresses, fighting each other for a chance to be penetrated by his frozen member while more whores and sorceresses try to bore their tongues into one of his many rectums, which are as numerous as the stars in the sky and evenly distributed around his body. Usually, however, they are consumed in the endeavor, digested and shat from another asshole into the fire.

Damned hags, screamed my guide or companion at the horny women. Even in Hell, you only want the most powerful and famous of the lot, completely oblivious of the pain it will cost you. You never think about anything other than stuffing that pink crevasse between your thighs with something monstrous and unholy that might spatter your womb with the germ of continuing wickedness in Hell as on earth

whether it's the sight of the robber biting the bishop's nose off or an unscrupulous prince ordering a massacre with a flick of his wrist from behind the walls of his fortress, regretting only that the sound of fighting disrupts his sleep, or the clown at the market, dazzling you with his obscene dancing, or a tub of lard with a wealthy father, like the one I've got in tow now as per the Lord's demand

it is always the stupidest, the meanest, the loudest scumbag in the crowd that has your lower lips dripping, longing to be crammed to the hilt with joy, filled with some atrocious sausage

protruding from a person who is not only sinful but also the absolute nequissimus

crudelis, obtusus, et lubidini obnoxius

and in this sorry person's arms you conceive your wailing litter, hollering the True King's name in your lust

and then you squeeze out what you conceived without a second thought, out of your crack and straight into the flames of eternal damnation, into the grinders and rolling mills of Hell, yelled my guide. He continued for a while longer in the same vein, for the lust of these women had truly enraged him

but I felt no inclination to raise my voice at any of the damned, not at these women attempting to charm and entice the great goat-bird in the flamepit, nor even at the great adversary himself. I cowered on the lamb's back, burying my face deeply in its wool.

I refuse to draw lessons from these visions, I said

and my guide thrust me off the lamb's back to the hard stone floor of the Antiherusalem tower from where we had witnessed the great opponent and the teeming smithies.

This tower shall be your mercy and your salvation, he bellowed. I've had to swear to the Lord not to harm you as I lead you through the true worlds

and the pain I am about to inflict will be subtracted from your final punishment, which will be measured out on a scale as unjust as the peddler's scale in the market square.

Every lash of the scourge you are about to experience will save you from a thousand after death, and you are undeserving of the mercy that will now rain down on your despicable back, sparing you the pain later.

But I can no longer contain myself and simply must beat you with my own hands, you are a disgrace to all things holy and I would tear you asunder and throw you into oblivion if the Lord would only let me. Now, you shall feel the burning scourge used by the angels toiling in Hell.

My guide stripped me of my cowl, my tunic, and my undergarments, leaving me naked on the hard stones of the Hell tower, ready to repent for my sins and all the foolish crimes I had committed in Iherusalem, in Antiherusalem, and on earth

indeed I even sinned on the back of the great fish in the world sea, which no one had ever done before me, probably

and he ordered me down on all fours like a donkey or a dog, or like the lamb you so stupidly feel kinship with.

Now he scourged my back and buttocks with the burning, six-thonged whip. No words can describe the sensation inflicted on my flesh by the angelic beating, and every time I tried to open my mouth to beg him for mercy, he only doubled down, causing my screams and wailing to overwhelm my pleas

and I thought that someone capable of such thorough flagellation could not possibly have been sent by the Lord

that he was monstrous, not angelic

and I contemplated how his flagellation was in violation of our monastery guidelines, which prescribe that there are several ways to punish with the whip, the scourge, or the cane. One can either punish oneself or be punished, and in the latter instance, it should be limited to the shoulders and the upper part of the back as it's considered inappropriate to apply the punishment to other areas of the body. Being undressed during the ordeal is strictly prohibited, as is, for that matter, being flogged on body parts that must always remain hidden

but every time I tried to remind my guide or my tormenter of this monastic rule, he only increased the fervor of his beating, lacerating my buttocks and testicles to the point where these, my shameful parts, felt reduced to mere shreds.

And while five of the burning thongs flogged my back, the sixth pierced through the frayed flesh of my destroyed behind like a gush of fire, twisting into my anus and up, up through my insides so I could feel it searing my bowels, then my stomach, and so on

before its crackling fire tip finally wound its way out my mouth in a stream of shredded, grilled organs, promptly dealing my face so many horrifying slaps it became striped with burning furrows like the rest of me, and this flaming tail I named Salvation.

Fling me into oblivion, Lord, I managed to scream, but my guide knew that the outburst was a lie, that I had still not given up my worldly inclinations, because he could tell that my flesh, even in this state, was ready to sin

and the sight of my readiness, poking out above my slashed scrotum and exposed testicles, still brimming with an idiotic zest for life, only made his beating more fervid.

Zilezzist

Another, final, flood of moaning from Gehrwas next to me. His healthy leg must have been dangling off the edge of the bed, stomping, and the sound of his sandal clacking against the floor was frantic and relentless as he wailed

Lord, is this it, is this it, Lord, Holy Wolfkang

an indeterminate sound interspersing his words, perhaps it came from his throat, not a squeak or a wail, it was more like a humming, a melodious stream unlike any sound I can remember.

The clacking sound from his healthy leg and his song of lamentation soon drowned out the voices of the geriatrics behind us

stop that racket, you're here for constipation, you're not at death's door, you've overeaten, you idiot, I've done it a thousand times

you've probably had too much of the sick's meat in the misericord, that'll teach you to usurp our privileges

pipe down, you're waking up the whole town.

None of them truly annoyed with him, but rather pleased, in fact, to have something to whine about. Before long, seven or eight of the old men were clamoring over each other, trying to shush down the young man who lay dying, each one of them thrilled to announce that they'd had it worse.

And it was only because Gehrwas's bed was right next to mine that I was still able to hear him, his lamentation and ceaseless clacking, through the yelling.

Pray for me, brothers, don't let me face Judgment alone, not without intercession. Your will be done, but I don't want to die like this, my life is in your hands, have mercy on me, Lord.

It didn't sound like he was addressing the noisy old brothers or the Lord anymore. The words flowed to the rhythm of his sandal's clacking, as if he were reciting a meaningless rhyme, and then he said the German prayer I taught him many years ago when he was a child and I had to give up sending him to school with the other children.

Trohtin almahtiger, tu der pist einiger trost

unta ewigiu heila aller dero

di in dih gloubant

iouh in dih gidingant

tu inluihta min herza

like an incantation to tether his soul to his twitching body. This is how I interpreted the apparition. The failed spell work of an anxious soul, stuttered words, losing their address and meaning, each syllable like a chunk ripped from the flesh of his throat.

Dina gnata megi anadenchin

unta mina sunta

In my heart, I prayed for Brother Gehrwas. That the three angels around my bed, whom I had never seen and whose comfort I had never felt, might watch over his bed instead of mine for a bit, for I was as certain as Gehrwas that the Lord was about to feed him to death, although no one besides the Lord knows the hour.

I prayed that the angel would dip his golden quill in golden ink and write an intercession on behalf of the crippled sinner on the page meant for me, who used to be his teacher, and that a choir of seraphs would sing this prayer in the Lord's presence

that the Lord would forgive his lies and delusions, that Saint Wolfkang would forgive him for slandering him, calling him a bog-reeking hermit

that he, in his naivety, would be spared the torments I had seen with my own eyes and be granted citizenship in the City of Heaven, be given his own tunic made of radiance and a strawberry wreath to wear around his head

that his leg, which on earth was withered and pained, and which he sinfully dragged toward the privy, would carry him in joyful sprints through the palace gardens where the head-bearing saints sing the Lord's praises.

Zilezzist piuiliho ih mih selhen

unta alla mina arbeita allen minen fliz in dina gnada

And I thought of the day we found him by the gate, a naked infant in the grass, a spring morning, I believe, his skinny leg ending in a nail-studded hunk of meat, flat in the grass while the other leg was twitching

was it his left leg or his right

when we found him, twenty or twenty-five years ago, he wasn't screaming

lay there with eyes filled with wonder, a dark gaze

it was only when Brother Heinrich took him into his arms that he began to scream.

Odo ni chunna

odo ni wella mih bidenchan duhr mina brodi

unta duhr mina unruocha

odo durb mina tumpheit

Whoreborn and abandoned and crippled and a constant nuisance in school. I only let him attend for a few days, then he was put to work to avoid the trouble that clung to him, the other boys wouldn't let him be. He asked me once if he could return, and I think I told him yes, if he could teach himself how to read first. Then I taught him the German prayer, a single day in the classroom together, I repeated it at least twenty times so that he would not be deprived of the chance for salvation, and he has listened and learned it by heart.

Unsa also din guita, unta din wistuom ist.

All this time I've listened to the sound of his leg being dragged through the corridors, and yet I can't recall whether it's the left leg or right that's withered. Even if I had been capable of asking him, I most likely wouldn't have, I would've prayed for him instead here at the point of death.

In manus tuas, Domine, commendo spiritum et corpus

The only Latin I taught him was that sentence, and it was the only one he needed now. But the Lord could rightly ask me why I never taught the boy to read the scriptures, seeing as he proved to be a fast learner.

In vain I scouted for a dark whirlwind or a degree of densification in the air above my bed that might indicate that my guide or companion was there to help me decipher the Lord's will from these meaningless movements in the half-perished world. But he was not here at the moment, and all I could glean from all this was that I had found Gehrwas as an infant, that I might have let him down during his childhood, and that he would now die as a young sinner while I listened to his cramps and cries, unable to offer him the slightest solace, and I drifted back into slumber before his death throes had subsided.

Here on Earth, and perhaps in the land of Necubia, too, there exists a kind of rest which is neither damned nor holy. In the dark square above me three stars hung in alignment as I awoke to the tolling of bells for Brother Gehrwas's soul, my thoughts still fixed on the boy I could've taught how to read.

The raven and the locust

We wound our way out of the dragon's mouth, Archipresbyter Werinharius and I, and with every step our thighs sank deeper into the dragon's tongue. Gooey bubbles erupted from the glands around us, bursting with a resounding pop akin to the shattering of a skull after a thousand years of plummeting through the throat beneath us.

I was pushing Archipresbyter Werinharius forward, yanking and pulling at his wool whenever he, in his exhaustion, paused and bleated glumly at me with his gaze lifted and his forehead lowered. For I had not forgotten the oath I had sworn to him a few days prior, riding toward the weaver's square in Hell.

My guide or companion floated merrily ahead of us, his laughter at my struggle to drag the reluctant lamb along echoing off the dragon's hollow teeth.

I could see light, but not a promising light. At first, on seeing the distant gleam, I was surprised that I could feel so indifferent about the sight of sunlight after several days in Hell City and a dreadful journey back up through the dark of the dragon's throat.

However, in the land Necubia, sunlight rarely sparks joy, and indeed this light seemed to me cold and gray like the waves of the world sea.

Feeling no particular relief, we walked the final stretch out of the dragon's mouth and could now gape at the dragon's foul head with the flaming snout, the armored scales, and the thirty horns without any wonder or terror whatsoever. In the dull light outside, Archipresbyter Werinharius even started licking the salt deposits on the monster's underlip blithely, though seemingly deriving no pleasure from it.

It's snowing, says the most tiresome of the old brothers. He has moved the bed that Gehrwas occupied last night and placed it against the wall to use as a platform to peer out the small window. He is wearing two lambskins, one on each shoulder, one yellowish and one black, resting his arms against the wall, blocking whatever heavenly rays might have been visible to us.

Look, it's snowing.

They're walking around down there now. You should see them. They won't get any work done on that wall today either. They're already slipping in the snow. Idiots.

Yes, you are idiots, I said. When you slide around in your sandals down there. What did you expect.

You slide like maids through a butcher's alley. You slide like turds through a dog.

He is standing completely still on the bed, resting his hands on the wall, his entire head sticking out the tiny window. Even through cowl and lambskins, I sense his sharp shoulder blades poking out of his scrawny back. The way he is standing, he is almost begging to have that kick in the ass which no one in this infirmary can administer.

Don't you stick out your tongue at me, or I'll show you how your mother likes it. Idiot. You're just skating around. Don't you have anything better to do. Don't you have anything better at all.

The dragon stared at us in moderate astonishment, clearly not used to seeing swallowed people coming back up, but not very interested either and definitely not aggressive to behold. Its large head protruded from the sandy gray soil, which stretched beyond our sight in every direction, with the occasional interruptions of small clusters of reeds and thorny shrubs.

My guide told me that we were now in the land of Necubia, and that on one side of us lay the region inhabited by the not very sinful, and to the other side, the part inhabited by the not very good. However, I no longer wished to hear what he had to say, and instead of waiting for him to finish his speech, I began dragging the exhausted lamb in the direction that looked to have the most vegetation, not concerned whether we were headed toward the slightly good or the slightly bad region. After many days in Hell, it seemed irrelevant.

Soon we saw a hilltop of a moldy green color. It wasn't too far away, and I patted my woolly fellow sufferer on his chest and pointed ahead.

Up there you'll be able to graze freely, my loyal Archipresbyter Werinharius, and that is where our paths must part, I said.

I had to push him most of the way up the hill, and once we arrived on the grassy top, I took his benevolent head in my arms, apologized again for all the hurt he had suffered, and let him graze. He bleated a discouraged farewell, then bent his head and started nibbling, sort of guiltily and without any great appetite, at the withered leaves of grass.

This was the last I saw of the lamb, I left him lonely on a hilltop in the realm of indifference.

At the foot of the hill lay a cluster of huts constructed from twigs and dung. In the center was a threshing floor, a barn, and a well, and behind these were uniform fields bearing a matte purple crop I had never seen before.

A group of people stood by the well and I shouted and waved my arms to attract their attention. They courteously returned my wave, and I thought to myself that they might be more on the not-so-good side rather than the not-so-bad, although perhaps there was no distinction to speak of, and I certainly wasn't planning to ask my guide about it. I was very content to be leading the party for once, although I knew it wouldn't be long before he robbed me of this one modest joy too.

With his head out the window, his butt in the air, and his elbows jutting out behind him, covered under the two lambskins, the skinny old brother in his matte black scapular reminds me of a talking raven I've met several times here in Recanespurch.

How much for the skin, it asked from behind the bars of its wicker cage, day in and day out. Its plumage was the same worn black as the old brother's scapular, its beak had turned gray, but its eyes held a deep, glossy darkness.

How much for the skin. Those might very well have been the last words spoken to me before I left town and they were certainly the first words I heard on returning five years later. The bird was still alive in its cage above the stand, but its feathers had faded to dusty gray and it still only asked the same foolish question. I don't recall how its owner looked, but I noticed the bird. Already then, the apparition of this bird seemed significant to me, as I dejectedly wound my way through the crowds of Recanespurch, the narrow alleys where all the wonders of the world that distract us from the Lord are bought and sold for gold and mutual damnation.

I had turned a corner and was standing face-to-face with the graying beast, the night bird, which no longer belonged entirely to the dark, that is how I interpret the apparition, and it asked me the price of a skin. I stopped and we studied each other with sidelong looks, heads tilted. It inquired one last time about the price of the skin. Then I proceeded toward Saint Emmeram's, where I knew I would spend the rest of my life, solitary and silent every day, unless to praise the Lord or to dictate mine and Heinrich's words from back then.

Now its shape reappears to me, and I hear its cawing in the old brother's ludicrous chatter on the bed. But what he is currently yelling at the brothers in the snow-filled yard lacks the gravity of the raven's inquiry back then. How much for the skin. What is the price of your skin, Brother. It had been asking the same question its entire life, but only in that moment, wandering down the alleys toward Saint Emmeram's to end my days where I have spent most of them in pious misery, did the raven's question make sense to me, this is how I interpret the apparition, and had it been in my power, with the Lord's blessing, and had I not forsworn speech, I would have broken my silence now, repeating the raven's question to the persistently yapping old man, whose scapular is no longer entirely of the dark, but whose heart and mouth are blacker than death.

How much for the skin, Brother, what was the price of your skin. For a bit of meat and the joy of listening to your own nonsense, you broke your promises to the Lord

promises, which might have secured you undeserved salvation and your own glorious robe in Heaven's Iherusalem. But I've seen a pack of dogs in Hell. They were eating a cartload of onions, waiting on the bell tower to bemoan your arrival, struggling to hold back their yellow shitwater. Is that a fair price for your skin, honored old brother.

Aw, shouts the old brother as he sits down with difficulty on the bed in front of me. There's no one left in the yard to shout at.

He is not raven-like viewed from the front. Straggly white hair reaches his cheeks and underneath, his square jaw juts out like a board with three rusty nails. His eyes are close-set and bloodred. But it seems as though the sight of him excludes the noise. Finally he stops talking.

He is sitting still, confused, wringing his hands in his lap across from me. His small red eyes are rolling in his head, as though scanning the room for something to talk about.

Then he leaps to his feet and points.

Hehe, what is that, what is that, he exclaims. A locust, look, a locust

there's a locust even though it's snowing.

It's on the edge of the bowl, he shouts.

I think it's going to eat his sloes.

You over there. If you even want your sloes. Do you realize there's a locust on the edge of your bowl.

I can't say whether it was a property of the land we found ourselves in, rendering everything indifferent, or if there was some other, hidden reason for my lack of joy at seeing Heinrich there, leaning over the old tree-trunk well in his black scapular, looking like himself, though somewhat more morose.

And maybe I did feel a kind of joy in that moment.

For it was as though my legs were preparing to run the final stretch downhill to him, and I thought that I would soon open my arms and fall on his neck, and I would tell him, as I often have in dreams, that I have never spoken to anyone since he left us. But something held me back or I caught myself. I fell back into my dejected ambling, which caused my guide or my tormenter to burst into scornful laughter, much as had happened on our journey before.

Glumly I greeted Heinrich and the five muddied peasants also standing around the well. None of them seemed keen on speaking with us or each other. Two of the peasants were engrossed in eating some of the large purple fruits that grew on the field behind us. They were gnawing the flesh from the bones of a foot and an underarm respectively, the juice from these limb-fruits dying their beards and Heinrich's smooth jaw bluish. Lividus is the name of the color, like the clouds or the cheeks of the hanged. The limb-fruits were the only edible crop that could grow in Necubia's sandy soil due to the land being Hellmouths's lid.

Don't I know you, said Heinrich, you seem familiar. His teeth and his tongue were also the blue of dead blood.

Soon, when the sun is at its highest, you will see it, he said. For that is what you have come to see, isn't it. I nodded. There's not much else to see anyway, he muttered

the holiest man I have ever met in a life spent among believers, he who walked to the Holy Land twice and returned once, who devoted his every moment to studies, prayer, and songs of praise

never letting his legs rest, his head find repose on a pillow, his belly indulge in wine and delectable food, he who cherished his linen tunic and his walking stick above everything else in the world

was now standing here, sentenced to gaze at a musty tree-trunk well, live in a dung-hut, and eat Necubia's bloody limb-fruits.

How much for the skin, Brother, I would have asked him, but he seemed to have already forgotten I was there. For the sun had now reached its highest point and was shining down the hollow trunk that served as the village well, and Heinrich and the other peasants leaned over the edge and gazed into it.

The infant in the well was Gehrwas, I recognized him at once. He lay silent and naked on his back in the water, arms splayed, legs paddling the dark water calmly, both the healthy leg and the stick-thin one with the club at the end. He looked up with the newborn's brooding gaze.

Not at us, but at the gray sky and the sundial above us. When finally sunlight filled the entire well, and only our heads still cast shadows along the rim, he began to speak in his young voice the German prayer I had once taught him,

Trohtin almahtiger, tu der pist einiger trost

unta ewigiu heila aller dero

di in dih gloubant

iouh in dih gidingant

tu inluihta min herza

The legs began twitching more violently in the water, arms plashing the surface as he cheeped the words of the prayer

Shine your light on my heart

Shine your light on my heart

addressing neither the Lord nor us the watchers, it was just a meaningless, broken invocation meant to enchant the sun's rays into staying in the well with him, never again leaving him to paddle in the dark.

New Directions Paperbooks—a partial listing

Adonis, Songs of Mihyar the Damascene
César Aira, Ghosts
   An Episode in the Life of a Landscape Painter
Ryunosuke Akutagawa, Kappa
Will Alexander, Refractive Africa
Osama Alomar, The Teeth of the Comb
Guillaume Apollinaire, Selected Writings
Jessica Au, Cold Enough for Snow
Paul Auster, The Red Notebook
Ingeborg Bachmann, Malina
Honoré de Balzac, Colonel Chabert
Djuna Barnes, Nightwood
Charles Baudelaire, The Flowers of Evil*
Bei Dao, City Gate, Open Up
Yevgenia Belorusets, Lucky Breaks
Rafael Bernal, His Name Was Death
Mei-Mei Berssenbrugge, Empathy
Max Blecher, Adventures in Immediate Irreality
Jorge Luis Borges, Labyrinths
   Seven Nights
Coral Bracho, Firefly Under the Tongue*
Kamau Brathwaite, Ancestors
Anne Carson, Glass, Irony & God
   Wrong Norma
Horacio Castellanos Moya, Senselessness
Camilo José Cela, Mazurka for Two Dead Men
Louis-Ferdinand Céline
   Death on the Installment Plan
   Journey to the End of the Night
Inger Christensen, alphabet
Julio Cortázar, Cronopios and Famas
Jonathan Creasy (ed.), Black Mountain Poems
Robert Creeley, If I Were Writing This
H.D., Selected Poems
Guy Davenport, 7 Greeks
Amparo Dávila, The Houseguest
Osamu Dazai, The Flowers of Buffoonery
   No Longer Human
   The Setting Sun
Anne de Marcken
   It Lasts Forever and Then It's Over
Helen DeWitt, The Last Samurai
   Some Trick
José Donoso, The Obscene Bird of Night
Robert Duncan, Selected Poems
Eça de Queirós, The Maias
Juan Emar, Yesterday
William Empson, 7 Types of Ambiguity
Mathias Énard, Compass
Shusaku Endo, Deep River
Jenny Erpenbeck, Go, Went, Gone
   Kairos
Lawrence Ferlinghetti
   A Coney Island of the Mind
Thalia Field, Personhood
F. Scott Fitzgerald, The Crack-Up
Rivka Galchen, Little Labors
Forrest Gander, Be With
Romain Gary, The Kites
Natalia Ginzburg, The Dry Heart
Henry Green, Concluding
Marlen Haushofer, The Wall
Victor Heringer, The Love of Singular Men
Felisberto Hernández, Piano Stories
Hermann Hesse, Siddhartha
Takashi Hiraide, The Guest Cat
Yoel Hoffmann, Moods
Susan Howe, My Emily Dickinson
   Concordance
Bohumil Hrabal, I Served the King of England
Qurratulain Hyder, River of Fire
Sonallah Ibrahim, That Smell
Rachel Ingalls, Mrs. Caliban
Christopher Isherwood, The Berlin Stories
Fleur Jaeggy, Sweet Days of Discipline
Alfred Jarry, Ubu Roi
B.S. Johnson, House Mother Normal
James Joyce, Stephen Hero
Franz Kafka, Amerika: The Man Who Disappeared
Yasunari Kawabata, Dandelions
Mieko Kanai, Mild Vertigo
John Keene, Counternarratives
Kim Hyesoon, Autobiography of Death
Heinrich von Kleist, Michael Kohlhaas
Taeko Kono, Toddler-Hunting
László Krasznahorkai, Satantango
   Seiobo There Below
Ágota Kristóf, The Illiterate
Eka Kurniawan, Beauty Is a Wound
Mme. de Lafayette, The Princess of Clèves
Lautréamont, Maldoror
Siegfried Lenz, The German Lesson
Alexander Lernet-Holenia, Count Luna

Denise Levertov, Selected Poems
Li Po, Selected Poems
Clarice Lispector, An Apprenticeship
   The Hour of the Star
   The Passion According to G. H.
Federico García Lorca, Selected Poems*
Nathaniel Mackey, Splay Anthem
Xavier de Maistre, Voyage Around My Room
Stéphane Mallarmé, Selected Poetry and Prose*
Javier Marías, Your Face Tomorrow (3 volumes)
Bernadette Mayer, Midwinter Day
Carson McCullers, The Member of the Wedding
Fernando Melchor, Hurricane Season
   Paradais
Thomas Merton, New Seeds of Contemplation
   The Way of Chuang Tzu
Henri Michaux, A Barbarian in Asia
Henry Miller, The Colossus of Maroussi
   Big Sur & the Oranges of Hieronymus Bosch
Yukio Mishima, Confessions of a Mask
   Death in Midsummer
Eugenio Montale, Selected Poems*
Vladimir Nabokov, Laughter in the Dark
Pablo Neruda, The Captain's Verses*
   Love Poems*
Charles Olson, Selected Writings
George Oppen, New Collected Poems
Wilfred Owen, Collected Poems
Hiroko Oyamada, The Hole
José Emilio Pacheco, Battles in the Desert
Michael Palmer, Little Elegies for Sister Satan
Nicanor Parra, Antipoems*
Boris Pasternak, Safe Conduct
Octavio Paz, Poems of Octavio Paz
Victor Pelevin, Omon Ra
Fernando Pessoa
   The Complete Works of Alberto Caeiro
Alejandra Pizarnik
   Extracting the Stone of Madness
Robert Plunket, My Search for Warren Harding
Ezra Pound, The Cantos
   New Selected Poems and Translations
Qian Zhongshu, Fortress Besieged
Raymond Queneau, Exercises in Style
Olga Ravn, The Employees
Herbert Read, The Green Child
Kenneth Rexroth, Selected Poems
Keith Ridgway, A Shock

Rainer Maria Rilke
   Poems from the Book of Hours
Arthur Rimbaud, Illuminations*
   A Season in Hell and The Drunken Boat*
Evelio Rosero, The Armies
Fran Ross, Oreo
Joseph Roth, The Emperor's Tomb
Raymond Roussel, Locus Solus
Ihara Saikaku, The Life of an Amorous Woman
Nathalie Sarraute, Tropisms
Jean-Paul Sartre, Nausea
Kathryn Scanlan, Kick the Latch
Delmore Schwartz
   In Dreams Begin Responsibilities
W. G. Sebald, The Emigrants
   The Rings of Saturn
Anne Serre, The Governesses
Patti Smith, Woolgathering
Stevie Smith, Best Poems
   Novel on Yellow Paper
Gary Snyder, Turtle Island
Muriel Spark, The Driver's Seat
   The Public Image
Maria Stepanova, In Memory of Memory
Wislawa Szymborska, How to Start Writing
Antonio Tabucchi, Pereira Maintains
Junichiro Tanizaki, The Maids
Yoko Tawada, The Emissary
   Scattered All over the Earth
Dylan Thomas, A Child's Christmas in Wales
   Collected Poems
Thuan, Chinatown
Rosemary Tonks, The Bloater
Tomas Tranströmer, The Great Enigma
Leonid Tsypkin, Summer in Baden-Baden
Tu Fu, Selected Poems
Elio Vittorini, Conversations in Sicily
Rosmarie Waldrop, The Nick of Time
Robert Walser, The Tanners
Eliot Weinberger, An Elemental Thing
   Nineteen Ways of Looking at Wang Wei
Nathanael West, The Day of the Locust
   Miss Lonelyhearts
Tennessee Williams, The Glass Menagerie
   A Streetcar Named Desire
William Carlos Williams, Selected Poems
Alexis Wright, Praiseworthy
Louis Zukofsky, "A"

*BILINGUAL EDITION

For a complete listing, request a free catalog from New Directions, 80 8th Avenue, New York, NY 10011 or visit us online at ndbooks.com